SAVED BY HIS HOOD LOVE

A Hood Romance

By
A.Lana

Saved By His Hood Love

Published by Alana's Book Line.

Synopsis

"You gotta closely watch these hoes. The bond that links your true family is not one of blood, but of respect and loyalty."-Aaliyah

"When you are deserving, you get the career, the friends, and the niggaz you want. A beautiful, deserving woman attracts nothing less than the best. However, weak jealous hoes don't understand that, and they try to interrupt your happiness." -Tokyo

Aaliyah and Tokyo Monroe are sisters. They're both doing their own thing as popular and successful women with bright futures, and they love it.
However, when passion, lust, envy, and narcissist behavior shows its face the sisters are faced with drama and chaos.

Tokyo can be the sister from hell and doesn't mind betraying others to get what she wants. Even her own sister.

Aaliyah loves hard and will never believe the people she loves the most would hurt her. She's blinded by love, and unfortunately it will cause her downfall.

Kash is the man and knows what he wants. Because of who he is, he always gets what he wants but some things are off limits.

Jersey is the one in the hood who hides his secrets well. None of the homies would ever suspect that he's who he is.

Saved By His Hood Love is supported by colorful characters and will have you entertained from beginning to end.

The Dedication

This book is dedicated to the chicks who are loyal to those they care about, and the hoes who betrayed them because of their own insecurities. To both sets of women, karma will always come back in full circle whether it's good or bad.

Tokyo

"What's up, baby daddy?" I spat mischievously as Jersey passed me in the hallway. He was headed into Aaliyah's room. As soon as the words left my mouth, he stopped dead in his tracks and stared at me. Even when he was mad, babe was handsome. Jersey put you in the mind of the R&B singer Chris Brown. He was fine and had a body that would have a bitch creaming in her panties just by looking at that broad chest and muscled ink-filled arms. The only difference was Jersey had long gold dreads that he wore hanging. I raised an eyebrow at the mug on his face and shifted my body weight on one side.

"Oh, so you mad now?" I pursed my lips. Shit, I was mad too. How was he just going to bring his ass in the house and go straight to that bitch's room without so much as acknowledging me? "How you mad at the truth?" I wanted to know. At the end of the day, I was his baby's momma and there wasn't a fucking thing he could do about it.

"You real messy. Too fucking immature. You fuck this off and you and that baby are dead to me. I put that on my dead momma." He warned.

'He never even met the crack head ho, but whatever.'

The way he looked at me with those dark brown eyes scared a bitch a little, but at the same time turned me on. My pussy got wet every time he was mad at me, but even wetter when we were fucking in the same house as him and his so-called girlfriend.

"Whatever, Jersey." I rolled my eyes, crossing my arms over my chest. He gave me the once over, and Jersey walked into Aaliyah's room.

I didn't bother to tell him she wasn't in there.

It was the first Tuesday of spring session, and she would be tutoring until later tonight.

Me, being the spoiled crazy bitch that I am, I stood in the hallway and began to undress. I took off my t-shirt and dropped it on the floor. The baby pink biker shorts came off too. At first, I was going to lay on the hallway floor and play in my pussy until he walked out of her room, but who knew when that would be.

Completely naked, I strolled into Aaliyah's room, leaving the door wide open. See, I didn't care about us getting caught. I was ready for him to tell her the truth, but he was prolonging it. He claimed it would benefit the both of us in the end. I knew one thing, he was running out of time.

When I entered the room, I wanted to gag at the pink and white décor Aaliyah had all over. The rug, vanity set, sheer curtains and comforter were either hot pink or white. The tramp swore she was a princess. That princess shit was so childish and overrated. I was Tokyo, the bad ass boss bitch. Fuck I look like walking around with princess shit.

Aaliyah's walk-in closet was open, so I knew Jersey was in there. I laid on the bed and began to finger myself; moaning loudly while thinking about him. The shit was feeling good.

"Girl, what you doing?" Jersey practically yelled. He was standing there with two duffle bags. With my sexy almond- shaped eyes, I stared at him in pure lust. I twirled my finger in and out of my dripping wet pussy.

"She won't be back until later." I whispered, never stopping what I was doing. I was on the verge of having an orgasm. I began to rotate my hips. I took my free hand and toyed with my hard nipple. Jersey had a smirk on his face. He looked at the door and then back at me.

"Come get your pussy before I-" my words were cut off. That nigga had jumped on top of me and had his big ass hand around my neck. He had the audacity to be upset that I wouldn't cut off my sidepieces when he was still with that bitch.

"You still wanna play? You giving that nigga my pussy?" He squeezed a little tighter. He was really choking me. Tears fell from the corners of my eyes as I tried to move his hand. My feelings were hurt more than anything. Jersey had never put his hands on me, no matter how slick my mouth got. "Are you still fucking that nigga?" He questioned, and I shook my head no. That's when he released the grip from around my neck.

Wham!

I slapped the shit out of him. I fucked with Jersey tough, but I wasn't with getting hands put on me.

"Stop playing with me so damn much." Jersey leaned down and forced his tongue inside of my mouth. Without hesitation, I welcomed it. We shared an aggressive kiss. And before I knew it, he was forcing his dick into my dripping wet pussy. Yes, I loved this toxic shit. What started as some freaky nasty shit between the two of us turned into a love triangle. At times, I hated my sister's man just as much as I loved him. However, I was tired of him prolonging us being a couple and raising our baby together.

Tokyo

It was the middle of the day. I was pushing my Benz AMG through the busy streets of L.A. It rained yesterday, but today it was 90 degrees with no dark clouds in the sky. Only in Cali. I was on my way to the office to meet up with a potential client. The chick who was interested in hiring me to make her a few pieces was referred by my sister. Aaliyah knew how I ran my business. When she referred people, they did meet the criteria I was looking for, but I still had to double-check before I agreed to a project. This girl Crystal didn't have any social media accounts that I could check out to see if she was a match for my clothes, so we had to meet in person.
You see, Tokyo Monroe just didn't sell her originals to any ole body. For me to fuck with you, you had to be somebody. I serviced bitches who were like me, BOSS BITCHES. What I look like letting a broke bitch sport my name? Hell, nah. My shit was top notch and expensive. Therefore, a broke hoe couldn't afford my shit. And I didn't care who didn't like it. I pride myself on my name and the items I make.

Let me back up a little. Again, I'm Tokyo Monroe. I'm 25 years old, the daughter of the late & famous rock star named Blair Monroe. My father died in a plane crash 14 years ago. He left my sister and I the house we were staying in now. Patricia, my mother, was one of my father's back up dancers and sidepiece. I thought I was the only child before he passed away. It wasn't until Daddy died that I found out that I had a sister two years older than me, Aaliyah. I was so pissed off at my father when I found out and more pissed at my momma when she left me at the gotdamn repast saying I had to stay with people I didn't even fucking know. Supposedly, she had to get her life together and didn't have the means to take care of me. So, I was left to be raised with my new sister by her momma. I didn't have an awful life. Miss Lori treated us both as a princess.

We lived on a prestigious crescent ranch estate in Perris, California. It had 4 bedrooms, 3 baths, with a large upstairs loft that was converted into a game room, and a 3 car garage. The mountain views were gorgeous. We had foreign whips, designer clothes, and kept fresh sneakers on our feet. She kept us in extra-curriculum activities and taught us at a young age the importance of knowing how to conduct business. She made us write a list of the things we liked and mark them from one to ten. She then made us write a story about what we saw ourselves doing as adults. She is part of the reason I am a fashion designer today. Like I said, it wasn't bad, but I still preferred to live with my own mother. My father left Momma nothing in the will to take care of me, and it left her depressed. She eventually turned to drugs. I always blamed Miss Lori and Aaliyah. It was those bitches fault. However, Momma is drug-free now, and she is back in my life. I'm doing what my daddy didn't, I take care of my mother.

It took me about an hour and ten minutes to get to my office. It was in the heart of downtown Los Angeles. The downtown LA area's traffic congestion was among the worst in the country. I had only been at my current location a year, but I loved it. It was a total upgrade from my previous office in the Crenshaw District. The location of any business spoke volumes. I went from having to walk to my car smelling loud weed smoke from the dudes who thought it was cool to loiter in an area where they paid no rent to something much nicer, an executive building.

I pulled into the valet and waited for the attendee to service me. Looking at my Cartier, I peeped I was twenty-nine minutes late. Oh well, she wanted my services, not the other way around. Grabbing my cellphone from the charger, I shot Crystal a text.

Me: Where are you?

Crystal: In the lobby.

Me: Sure thing. I'm coming in.

Crystal: Thanks.
I rolled my eyes. *Girl please,* I thought sensing she had an attitude.

Just as the valet approached my door, my cellphone rang. I sighed when I saw my momma's name appear on my screen.

“Hey, Ma.” I said. I already knew she was calling for one of three things: to complain, talk shit about somebody, or remind me about the BBQ she was throwing.

“Don’t hey Ma me like I’m bothering you.” She snapped. The TV in the background was loud enough to wake the dead. I swear she acted as if she was deaf as a stone.

“I ain’t acting like nothing. I just pulled up to work and I have a client waiting.”

“Let the bitch wait. She wants your services. The fuck.”
I laughed. Ma had no filter, and I was just like her.

“True. What’s up, though?” I asked.
A tap on my window made me snap my head to the left. I frowned up my face at the valet attendant. A tall Latino guy. He was letting me know he was ready to move my car.

“Give me a minute.” I rolled my eyes.

“I know that ain’t your client, girl?” My ma asked.

“No. It’s the low-paid valet guy. Anyway, what’s up, Ma?”
I looked straight ahead. My ignore game was on 100.

“I was calling to tell you your father’s lawyer called me. He wanted Aaliyah’s number. I asked him why, but he said it was confidential. I told him to find her ass himself then and hung up. I wonder what he wants with her. Has he called you?”
I thought about it for a minute. Early this morning, I checked all of my most recent messages and emails.

"No, he hasn't." Instantly I felt some kind of way. If Daddy's lawyer was reaching out, it was money involved. *So why hasn't he called me?* Let me find out some sneaky stuff was going on; I swear it was going to be problems.
"Well, keep your eyes and ears open. I wanna know what the fuck is going on."

"You and me both." I countered.

"I will see you on Saturday. I'm going to text you the list of what I need, or you can just send me the money."

"Girl, bye. I'll send you the money. Oh, Momma. Can you tell Auntie Nita that I need her to write me up a positive pregnancy test?"

"Bitch, what you got going on?" She laughed.

"Tell you later, bye." I hung up.
Although my mom got on my nerves, she was my best friend. Patricia Santos taught me everything I knew when it came to surviving in a world where everybody wanna be somebody and will step on their own grandma to get there. She taught me that I come first and there was no hoe alive above me. She taught me to set my standards high and accept nothing less than what I wanted. And how to get it by any means necessary. Life without her wouldn't be right. Patricia didn't tolerate bullshit and at 47, she was still a real one.

Pulling my sun visor down, I looked at my reflection in the mirror. I loved my sexy chocolate ass. I was a cute bitch. I got it from my momma. My silky long jet-black hair and full lips were inherited from my dad. I knew I was cute and heard it often. Sexy chocolate is what they called me.

Grabbing my Fendi purse from the backseat, I fished around inside and pulled out my makeup bag. After applying another coat of lip-gloss, I gathered my things and exited the truck.

Walking up to the building, I stared at my reflection in the mirror entrance the entire time. *'Tokyo you bad.'* I said to myself. I admired my curvy figure in a white Polo Ralph Lauren belted knee-length dress. A bitch's body was flawless. Nothing on me was fake. Like my momma, I've always had the perfect shape, a handful of breasts, an ironing board flat stomach, wide hips, smooth long legs and an ass that shook like a bowl of jelly. *'Got damn you look good. These bitches ain't got shit on you.'* My ego was always gassing me up. I loved her. My ego was a whole person.

My 7-inch YSL clear strap heeled sandals click-clacked on the marble tile as I made my way to the waiting room. I smiled at the security guard and waved at the twins as they walked by. They were two white chicks whose law office was in the building.

"Tokyo." One of them called my name, and I turned around. I smiled.
"Yes."
"I didn't know Aaliyah was your sister. We were having drinks, and she brought you up. She recommended you to a mutual friend. She said her sister can make her an original wedding dress shutting down all top designers."
"My sister is right. She should reach out." I replied.
"I'm not sure if she will, but your sister praised your work and highly recommended you. She showed pictures and all. She made me want to hire you." She laughed.
"That's my sister." I said.
"She's a sweetie. See you later." She gave me the once over. "I love those shoes." With that, she walked off. The other twin smiled and continued on as well.

"Hi, Crystal." I spoke to a bi-racial chick sitting in the lobby. She was the only one there, so I knew it was my client. While tapping away on her cellphone, she put up one finger. It offended me immediately. I wanted to check her ass and let her know that it was time to get down to business, but I was late. I was going to tax the shit out of her ass, though. She finished with the text and tossed her phone in her oversized designer bag. *'Damn.'* I thought. I wanted that bag. I wanted to ask where she got it, but I wasn't about to come off as thirsty.

Crystal stood up and looked at me up and down, and I returned the gesture.

I could tell she had money or a sponsor with paper. The Dior bag she rocked wasn't even out yet. She was dressed in a fitted lime green T-shirt, white Montclair biker shorts, and black 10-inch Louboutins heels, and she looked cute. The bitch had on a bust down and a diamond ring on her middle finger that was at least five carats. I didn't know if she had plastic surgery done to her body, but she was bad. I could hang with her. I bet she knew where the rich niggas be.

'Maybe we can be friends.' I thought.

"Tokyo." She stared. "I am Eva Sinclair. I am not Crystal. I am a celebrity stylist. Your sister tutors my niece. Long story short, she suggested your company. I went on your IG, and I love your work. I thought my clients would too. However, my clients are very serious about their money and cautious about who they do business with. Your business etiquette is horrible. It's an embarrassment. I know you probably don't care. You have a great following, but to move up in this industry and do business with influential people who are movers and shakers you have to change some things. I have a few suggestions for you. You should make sure you're knowledgeable about the clothing industry. Get an understanding of how the business works. Read about how other brands became successful and model a similar strategy."

"Bitch, fuck you." I wanted to say. I was heated. That hoe straight trash talked me. "I don't need shit you have to offer. I'm doing good. Real damn good." I put my hand on my hip.

"Good for you. Have a nice day, Ms. Monroe." With that, she walked out. I wanted to drag that broad so bad. What kind of bullshit was she on? Stupid bitch.

Kash

"Yeah. I just pulled up. I know, Pops. I got this." I said into the phone, trying my best to hide my annoyance. I loved my OG despite his shortcomings, but Cuz stayed getting on my nerves. Nothing irked me more than a person trying to dictate how I moved. As I sat in my all-white Benz with the limo tinted bulletproofed windows, I stared at The University of Southern California's sign. I drowned out my pops, repeating over and over again how important this play was. I sat up in my seat when her black Audi pulled next to me.

"She's here, Pops. Later." I said, hanging up the phone. I knew he was cussing my ass out for the way I just hung up like that, but shit we had nothing else to talk about. I wasn't going to answer any more of his calls until I was ready to make that move.

I watched as Ms. Aaliyah dropped her sun visor and applied her lipstick. She sprayed on some perfume and then lotioned herself down. I cracked a smile, thinking she was doing the extras just for me. Finally, she stepped out of the car. Taking the thick-ass woman in, I couldn't help but admire how good she looked in a curve-hugging orange tube- top dress. Miss Aaliyah stood about 5'5, she carried weight in all the right places- big round titties and a fat ass. She had a little FUPA she would try to hide by putting her hand right there at times. I'm sure that's why she was always rocking a fanny pack to hide her little pouch. In my eyes, she was perfect. The short blonde bob she rocked enhanced her butter toffee complexion. The sunlight glistening on her, showed off the shimmering gold spray on her upper body. I was in a relationship, and I loved my girl, but I couldn't help but lust for Aaliyah every chance I got. I watched as she walked to her trunk and pulled out her backpack.

Two females in a yellow bug pulled up and hopped out of the car.

I was sure baby girl was about to be caught slipping. I didn't get in females shit, but I be damn if I let baby girl get packed out. I watched. A big smile spread across my face and a nigga felt proud when I saw Miss Aaliyah come out of the trunk with a .38 revolver. I guess I underestimated her. The bitches didn't even see it until she had the chrome aimed at their dome pieces.

"I saw you hoes following me in this ugly ass car. I'm going to tell you like this, I don't play fair. So, what's up?" Aaliyah challenged.

"Your scary-ass got that gun, that's why you hard. But this ain't even about you." The girl who was driving said.

"I'll use this bitch too." Aaliyah shot back.

"I want you to deliver this message to your grimy ass sister. Tell her whenever I see her, I am going to drag her ass. Tell your sister she can keep fucking your man and your stupid ass is too blind to see it, but I ain't stupid. Tell her to stay the fuck away from mine. Bitch blocked me from her IG and Twitter." The driver said. The other chick just stood there with her phone out like she was ready to record.

"You tell her." Aaliyah tossed back.

"I am. But you see how I just told you she was fucking your man, and you ain't said shit about that. They both know you're dumb."

"Girl, gone. And take your fake ass news with you." Aaliyah retorted. I guess she knew they didn't want any static because she put the gun into her backpack. I was ready to pop off if the bitches tried to be slick. Both girls called her a few stupid bitches before they jumped back in their car and pulled off. After she gathered her things from the car, she shut her trunk and ambled up to my passenger window, using her long nude colored nails to tap on the window.

"You got five minutes. If you are even a minute late, I'm out." She tossed over her shoulder. She didn't know that gangsta shit turned me on. *"Focus, Kash. Focus."* I said as I watched her head to the building we'd meet in for tutoring.

I sat there for a few seconds before running after her.

"Aye, Miss Aaliyah." I called behind her, but she didn't stop. When

I finally caught up, I grabbed her by her hand. She stopped in her tracks and looked at me with annoyance all over her face.

"Look, I can tell your energy is off. How about we ditch this session and go grab some ice cream?" I smiled at her.

"I love ice cream. Thank you for the offer. However, that is not a good idea, Mr. Bryant." I took my bottom lip into my mouth as I took her in for the second time today. The way my name would roll off her tongue had a nigga's dick hard every time. I had a bitch, but it was something about Aaliyah's innocence but confidence that had me digging her.

"Stop doing that." I demanded.

"What?" She raised a brow.

"Saying my name like that. You're going to get yourself into some trouble." She shook her head and removed her hand from mine. I glimpsed her sexy ass blushing, though. "What's your favorite ice cream?" She smiled before answering me.

"Chocolate Malted Crunch when I'm on my period and pineapple sherbet when I'm not. Well, anything sherbet."

"I fuck with anything sherbet too. Let's get some."

"How many times do I have to tell you I don't go on dates with my clients and I have a boyfriend?" She questioned with her hand on her hip.

"The one they just accused your sister of fucking? You ain't talking about him, right?"

"Boy, fuck you and mind the business that pays you. Better yet, work on getting that D up. That's all you need to be worried about right now." With that, she continued towards the building where she tutored.

'Damn.'

I ran back to my car and grabbed my gun from the center console, secured it in my waist and then put my backpack on one shoulder. She was right. I only had two months to get my D in history up to at least a B, or I was going to lose my football scholarship.

I'm Kash Bryant. The cocky bougie nigga with a lot of money and talent. I was born into wealth. My father, Mr. L.A. was one of the biggest hustlers in Southern California. He was the heroin plug. You would think his gangster lifestyle as a drug kingpin would be his downfall, but negative. Pops was on the run now living in Mexico for murder, conspiracy to commit murder, and some other shit. He had the money to hire a skilled lawyer, but he didn't feel that was enough to prevent him from serving a long bid. Pops fucked around and fell in love with a politician's wife. When the wife divorced her husband for Dad, shit hit the fan and old girl's husband was killed. Of course, they blamed it on my father.

I was 17 when Pops fled the country. I missed my pops. We had the perfect relationship, but I will always hold animosity against him for how he up and bounced. Yeah, I had my mom, and my sister would be home to celebrate my draft to the NFL–it was coming, but even at 19, I wanted my pops. That shit mattered. I wanted him here.

Aaliyah

I was exhausted after tutoring my three clients, but I loved it. I took great pleasure in contributing to the success of others. On the drive home, all I could think about was a hot shower. My stomach growled. I could hardly wait to get home to cook a homemade burger on sliced bread, with extra mustard, and topped with a slice of cheddar cheese. What a way to end a long day. I felt like even indulging in a good book until I drifted off to sleep.

When I pulled up to the house I shared with my sister, I was instantly annoyed. There were three cars in the driveway. So, not only did I have to park on the street, but I would have to deal with her having company. I mentally prepared myself for the smell of weed smoke, blunts circulating around from one person to another, loud rap music and loud talking. My sister partied more than she slept. She lived to turn up and kick it all day and all night long. Me on the other hand, I was more of a reserved person.

Let me properly introduce myself. I'm Aaliyah Monroe, and I'm 27 years old. I attended USC, after deciding to further my education. I was in one of the most prestigious large private universities in Southern California where I'm studying to obtain a Bachelor's degree in Business Administration. Not only that, but I'm a huge makeup lover. Although I don't wear much, I take great pleasure in beautifying others. Between school, my gig tutoring, and my future husband Jersey, I don't have time to try my hand at profiting from doing makeup. My boyfriend believes I'm so good I can become big in the industry. That is why I loved Jersey, he stayed supporting me. He says with my talent and the connections I have by being the daughter of Blair Monroe, I could be famous. Tokyo and I share the same father. Our father was a famous musician. He passed away when I was young. Neither of us knew we had a sister until Daddy died. When I got older, I found out that our mothers knew about each other and each other's kid from day one. My mother is Liza Monroe. By the way, she never remarried. Said she found out about Tokyo when her mom was pregnant with her. Tokyo's mom refused to allow my sister and I to have a relationship. That was, until Daddy died and left her with nothing. She left her own daughter to be raised by a stranger. Luckily, Momma is good people and loved us the same. I really believe Tokyo feels some kind of way about that. I don't see how, when my mother gave her everything she gave me except life. My mother didn't have to do what she did for Tokyo, but she did.

At times, Tokyo could be so damn selfish. I loved my sister, but there was only so much I could take. I couldn't wait until I graduated. She could have this house. I was moving to The A to be with my mom and my man was coming with me.

When I walked into the house, it was just what I expected. Weed smoke hit me smack in the face. To my surprise, the music wasn't on. It wasn't until I made it all the way inside that I saw my sister and two of her friends in the living room looking over fabric. My sister is a self-proclaimed fashion designer. She would make custom pieces for the uppity wanna-be boss chicks from different states.

"Hey." I spoke and everyone but my sister spoke back. She killed me with her funny acting attitude. The tramp was always mad. Like, damn. I knew she was getting dick because she was forever letting it be known when her nigga dicked her down. Speaking of that, I called her name, and she looked at me like she was annoyed. "Come here, I gotta tell you what happened today." I told her and headed to the kitchen.

"What, Fats?" I hated the nickname she gave me, and she knew it but whatever.

"Why some bitch with her home girl rolled up on me today? Said that you were fucking her man and mine. She said she's going to

beat your ass when she sees you."
"And what you do or say? Did you have my back?"
"I pulled out my gun. She said she just wanted me to deliver the message and got mad when I didn't address her claiming that you are fucking my man. They were in a yellow bug."
"Oh, that's the hoe that used to dance at Secret Sundayz. Dusty ass hoes." I shook my head because she was always into some mess. Just like her to be unbothered. "But, why this bitch Eva Sinclair dissed me? Said you told her niece about me. I was about to whoop her ass. I made Tokyo. Can't no bitch take credit for where I am at. I don't need her."

I had to blink a few times. Eva was the plug. She had connections. I knew Tokyo, she just didn't like anyone telling her what to do. That was her damn problem. I didn't even say shit when she walked out. I didn't have time.

After making sure the ground beef I took out was still at the bottom of the fridge and thawed, I quickly seasoned it and put it back in the fridge. I then ran to my room to grab my things to shower. Before climbing in the shower, I put my dead cellphone on the charger. When I got out of the shower, I had quite a few text messages. My boyfriend Jersey text letting me know that he was halfway to Fresno, and he would call me when he got there. There was a message from my mom and big cousin. I quickly replied to them, letting them know I was home, and I would call them on my way to class. A few clients text confirming for next weeks tutoring, but I wouldn't reply until morning. I took pride in my professionalism. Mr. Bryant, my client was trying to break my rules, but I wouldn't allow it. It was a shame how I couldn't stop smiling when I read Mr. Bryant's text.
Mr. Bryant: I apologize for how I got at you today. However, you hurt my feelings when you wouldn't go get ice cream with me. (Sad face).
Me: Apology accepted. I cannot mix personal and business.
Mr. Bryant: What if I find another tutor? Can I take you out then?

Me: Go to sleep. You're stuck with me until you pass this class.
Mr. Bryant: I like the sound of that. Good night, Ms. Aaliyah.
Putting the phone down, I laid back on the bed. I thought about the chicks that pulled up on me today. I then thought about how old girl claimed my sister was fucking my man. I knew Jersey would never do me like that. We've been together for two years, and it has been perfect from day one. Besides him being in the streets, I had never had a reason to question his loyalty. Nevertheless, I couldn't help it. I texted him.
Me: Some chick tried to run up on me. Talking about, I need to tell Tokyo to stay away from her man. Oh, and she told me I was dumb because Tokyo is fucking my man too.

He texted right back.

Babe: I can't wait until we move. Your sister is always into some shit. She will fuck around and get somebody hurt. SMH. I ain't even going to address that other shit.
Me: I can't wait until we move, either. I love you.
Babe: I love you, too. Now, go eat something and go to sleep. I will call you in the morning. Goodnight.
Me: I'll be waiting for your call. Be safe. Goodnight.

I wanted to get up and make my burger so bad, but my body didn't want to move. Fuck that burger. I didn't need it anyway. As the sandman took over my eyes, thoughts of my sister and man fucking resurfaced. I quickly reminded myself that Jersey wouldn't do me like that. I felt bad afterwards for questioning his trustworthiness.

Flashback

I was sitting on the porch enjoying the cool breeze. I had a cup of lemonade in one hand and a book in the other. Since my sister was sleeping, I'd taken my small boom box on the porch with me to listen to music. I had been outside chilling for a cool minute before I got hungry and decided to go make me something to eat. Just as I was about to get up, Money Mike pulled up in the driveway. His music was loud as usual. I cut my eyes at him. It had been three hours since my sister had made it home, and his ass was just now coming to check on her.

Mike stepped out the car as usual, dressed to impress. Designer jeans, shirt, and a pair of Jordon sneakers completed his fit. Money Mike was very handsome. Dark chocolate, medium built with just enough muscle to show off his ink filled arms. Aside from being good-looking, he was the man in the city with money. My sister stayed getting into it with other females over him, but that wife she could never contact, Mike made sure of that. A small smile formed on my face when he stepped out the car. He had two Nike bags in one hand and a Macy's bag in the other. He was always spoiling my sister.

"What's up, big head?" He spoke.

"It's been three hours, and you are just now showing up. Just like you to bring gifts to make up for your fuckups." I looked at him in disgust.

"Damn, little sis. It's like that?" He looked at me shocked and I rolled my eyes. Mike was always on some disappearing shit. He was probably with his wife. I knew he loved my sister, but he loved his wife and what he was doing in the streets more.

"Where my baby at?" He asked, looking towards the house.

"I'm sure sleep. She went through a lot."

"What are you talking about?"

"Mike, she had her procedure today. She said you were supposed to take her, but I had to."

"What are you talking about?"

"The abortion, stop playing stupid." The way he looked at me told me I fucked up.

"Abortion? She had a fucking abortion?" His response confirmed it.

"You didn't know?" I asked. Tokyo lied to me. She ain't tell the man. She knew I didn't believe in abortions, but convinced me to take her.

"Please don't tell her I told you." Mike shook his head.

It was her fault I slipped up, but she would blame me.

"Don't trip. I ain't going to say shit." With that, he walked into the house. Not even five minutes later, he came back out without the bags and scurried out of the driveway. He didn't even say bye. He was mad.

I sat there, praying Mike didn't rat me out like I had done my sister.

It was around 10 o'clock at night when I got a call from an old friend inviting me out to a party. I wasn't into parties like that, but this summer I vowed to have fun. Luckily, Mike hadn't told my sister that I told her business. So, that put me in a good mood, which is another reason why I went out.

The party was lit. I was drinking and dancing. Dancing was second nature to me. I always cut up on the dance floor.

I was really having a good time, so much of a good time that I got drunk. I was standing by the bar drinking a bottle of water and bobbing my head to the music when Mike walked up asking me if I wanted another drink. I told him I did.

I remember my friend telling me that she was going to afterhours and Mike offering to take me home.

"Why are we at the motel?" I remember asking, and then everything went black. The next time I opened my eyes, we were inside the motel.

"Mike, it's hot. I need to shower."

"Come on. Let me show you where it's at." The last thing I remembered

was moaning while Mike fingered me in the middle of the bathroom.

He sent a video to Tokyo. It was the same video Tokyo took upon herself to send in a group chat that included our moms. Even after she confronted me about it, she sent the video to them.

It showed me standing in the hotel naked while I seduced Mike. I gave him oral sex, rode him like a stallion and told him how he should've chosen me.

I didn't remember none of that shit. My mom instantly suspected him of drugging me. When I went to the hospital, I had a date rape drug in my system. It was the prescription pill known as benzodiazepine. It's chemically similar to drugs such as Valium or Xanax. The blood tests results confirmed my mother's suspicions. I still didn't press charges. I let it go. My mom and I prayed for God to handle it. My sister even forgave me. Six months later, Mike was killed coming out of a liquor store by the cops. It was mistaken ID.

Tokyo never brought it up, but what I didn't like was how sometimes she would share stories about her and Mike and how she missed him. It was like a slap in the face. I knew she held ill feelings towards me for what happened, but I hoped she never reacted on them.

Aaliyah -Present

I was all smiles after receiving a text from my baby Jersey telling me to pack my bags. He had a surprise for me. He was coming to pick me up.

I knew he made it back in town, but between my classes and not wanting to bother him, I patiently waited for him to reach out first.

I had just pulled up to Walmart when I got the text. I was about to go in and grab a few items and some more ground beef because I forgot to take some out of the freezer before I left for class. I could throw down when it came to cooking those homemade juicy burgers. Mine were so darn good. My mouth watered every time I thought about it. I wanted another one. Hands down, homemade burgers are always the best. However, since Jersey said he'd be picking me up in less than an hour I drove off the parking lot and headed home. Damn, I wanted that burger. However, I wanted to spend time with my man more. Instantly, I felt the "butterflies in the stomach" feeling the moment I thought about Jersey. He was everything to me. Not only was he handsome, but he was the perfect boyfriend. He always put me first. He never missed an opportunity to tell me how much he loved and appreciated me.

This was my first serious relationship. I dated here and there, but Jersey was my first when it came to things that mattered. He was my first thug. He was the first man that I ever had oral sex with, and the first I would give my life for. I was somewhat old fashioned for my age when it came to relationships. I didn't have sex on the first date, and I always let guys ask me out first. After the date rape, I waited a couple of years before I decided to go out with anybody. It mentally bruised me and gave me deep trust issues, but I trusted Jersey with my heart and soul. He made me feel excited, anxious, complete, and totally in love. I couldn't imagine a love stronger than what I felt with him.

The day we met...

I was coming out of Starbucks. I was busy texting Tokyo, well, arguing with her about something stupid when I ran smack into the back of his vehicle. Just as fast as I looked up, his thug ass was jumping out of his black truck with a scowl on his face checking his vehicle for damage. I went to reach for my purse to grab my mace- just in case he tried to hit me- he looked that mad. Before I could get the mace, he snatched the door open.
"I apologize." I said. I was really sorry and afraid. However, I couldn't help but to notice how damn fine he was. A designer shirt with semi baggy pants displaying boxers wasn't attractive to me, but he made it look good.
"How you just gon' hit my shit and apologize? That's it?" He asked, with a smirk on his face.
I peeped how he studied my face before looking at my boobs and my thighs that hung out of my shorts.
"I have insurance. They will pay to have the damage repaired." I looked at his truck and didn't see any damage. I didn't say anything, but knew that's why he wasn't tripping about me hitting him.
"Fuck all that. I want your number. You gotta let me take you out." His frown was gone and replaced by a crooked smile.

"Are you serious?" Security walked up, stealing our attention. Jersey didn't appreciate it.
"The fuck you want? Do it look like we need your services? Move around. I'm talking to my future girl."
I shook my head at his silliness.
Turning from the security, he looked back at me.
"Give me your phone." I didn't hesitate to hand it over. He called himself from it and then handed it back to me. "Stay on the line. We are about to talk about our date." He ordered. Before he walked away, he asked me was I ok. I told him yes, and he got in his truck. We talked until I made it home. Later that night, we talked some more. The next

day we were on a date and two years later, we are still together.

**

I hopped on the freeway and into the FasTrak, which allowed some commuters to bypass the heavy traffic. The sky was a hue of red and orange. It was beautiful watching the sunset.

Jersey and I made it to my house at the same time. I hadn't seen my man in two days. I quickly jumped out of the car wearing the biggest smile. He climbed out of his ride and I ran to him, wrapping my arms around his neck.

"What's up, babe?" He pulled back and kissed me. With ease, I slipped my tongue into his mouth, and we shared a long passionate kiss. God, I loved this man. Jersey tapped me on my butt.

"Go pack. I gotta make a few calls."

"Ok." I countered and strolled into the house.

Jersey

Fucking two sisters was a gotdamn headache. I felt guilty about my betrayal more than I had this past year. Especially since the hoe Tokyo was saying she was pregnant by me. I knew for a fact that once we left Cali, I could break all ties with Tokyo. As long as I was still here, and Aaliyah shared a home with her sister, me and Tokyo would end up fucking again. I hated that shit. I got mad at the homie today because he called me scandalous, claiming I was selfish and really didn't love my bitch. He acted like he wanted to fuck her.

I lied when I told Aaliyah that I was going to wait in the car and make a few calls. I just didn't want to go inside. If Tokyo showed up while I was inside, she would be on some spiteful shit. She'd make petty ass comments to make me mad, but at the same time try to give Aaliyah a hint. I hated that bitch sometimes.

When Aaliyah told me some hoes rolled up on her about Tokyo and tried to convince her that me and Tokyo were playing her, I truly believed that Tokyo set that shit up. I was pissed off. I called the bitch too and she neither denied nor admitted to it. Talking about, my concern should be our child. Like the homie said, if she was pregnant, the baby probably wasn't even mine. Thinking about the shit gave me a headache. I wish I would've never started fucking her ass. The hoe didn't know how to be a peaceful side-bitch. She was spiteful and evil.

Tap Tap ...

I was scrolling on IG when the tapping on my window got my attention. I was annoyed as fuck when I saw it was Tokyo. Standing there with her lips pursed and arms folded like she had an attitude.

Reluctantly, I rolled my window down.

"What?" I asked.

"Why you out here?"

"Waiting on Aaliyah. You straight?" I couldn't really snap on the hoe like I wanted to. Her ass would be quick to make a scene.

"What y'all about to do?" After the question left her mouth, Aaliyah came strolling out the house with her overnight bag. I looked from Aaliyah to Tokyo, and she had a frown on her face.

"What's wrong with you?" Aaliyah asked.

Tokyo looked at me, then back at Aaliyah and smirked.

"Nothing's wrong. Y'all have fun." She strolled off. I knew she was fuming.

When we pulled up to the hotel, Aaliyah's eyes brightened and the huge smile on her face made me feel good. I remembered her saying how she wanted to visit the hotel one day because it sat on the ocean.

My girl deserved this and more. She was a good girl with a beautiful soul.

"Wow. I love this." Aaliyah said as she walked out of the hotel suite and on to the patio. "This view is amazing. I can sit out here all night." She complimented as she looked at the ocean.

"I thought it was nice too. I remembered you telling me that you wanted to come here." I put my arms around her waist and kissed her on the cheek. With my mouth up to her ear I whispered. "Can I get some pussy out here?"

Aaliyah giggled. She turned around. Resting up against the rail, she wrapped her arms around my neck.

"You can have me anywhere and any place." She replied with so much sincerity that my heart beat quickened. Aaliyah was the girlfriend everyone loved. People would often tell me how lucky I was to have her. The way she looked at me while giving me permission to have control over her did something to me. It made me realize how much in love I was with my girl, and how I needed to get my shit right.

"I love you." I told her before planting a wet kiss on her full bubble gum flavored lips. Aaliyah slid her tongue in my mouth and my dick got harder than it was. My hands caressed her soft heart shaped bottom as our tongues slow danced to its own tune. I was just about to hike up her dress and fuck her right there, but the knock on the door put a temporary stop to us fucking. Breaking our kiss, I let Aaliyah know what was up.

"That's room service."

She smiled.

"Awww, baby. So sweet."

The way she beamed made a nigga's chest swell.

Tokyo

"Bitch, be ready by 10 o'clock or your ass ain't coming." I was on FaceTime with my friend Lori. I invited her to come to this party with me. It was a spur of the moment and Lori was one of my girls I knew would be down to come. I was going to this party with a goal in mind, and wasn't no hoe that's always trying to compete going to get in the way of me snagging Kash. That's why I didn't invite my other home girl.

I was really feeling Jersey, but it wasn't nothing for me to leave him for a nigga that wanted me. And who had way more paper.

"I'll be ready later, friend." Lori said, ending our FaceTime. Tonight Kash was having a party. It was a party for his big sister. Word on the street was she did a bid for her man and after 16 months, she was home. I didn't tell Lori, but I wasn't personally invited.

I left the office and decided to hit the bar for happy hour and overheard the conversation between the waitress and bartender. Those hoes were running their mouths so much, if I was an OPP it would've been my lucky day. At first, I didn't really care about the shit they were gossiping about. We were of a different caliber, but when I heard Kash's mansion party my ears perked. Kash was a big baller. Everybody and their momma wanted to be around him and I was one of them. Thanks to those gossiping hoes, I knew what time the party was, where the mansion was located, and who was performing.

We arrived at the party around 11 o'clock. Everybody and their mamas were there. From the nobody's to the somebody's, everyone mingled together. I ain't going to lie, it was some fine niggas and bad bitches in the building. They weren't my business, though. I was looking for Kash, not one bitch on earth could hold a candle to me, and I meant that. Donned in a white sheer two-piece Tokyo Monroe original, my thousand-dollar designer heels clickity-clacked all around the party as I sashayed. Lori was right behind me. Although I looked better, Lori was looking like a bad bitch too. She was shitting on hoes rocking a black cropped shirt that showed a flat tummy, ghost-white colored Gucci denim hot shorts and a pair of black Givenchy thigh boots. Lori was one of those high yellow chicks with gray eyes. She was a bag chaser like me. However, she loved pussy. That's another reason I invited her. I didn't have to worry about her getting at Kash.

The bartender had just handed Lori and I our drinks when the DJ spoke into the mic. Lori and I looked towards the stage in the middle of the yard. "I would like to give a warm welcome to every-

one who came out tonight. Let's party all night long." While everyone drank and danced, I eye searched the crowd for Kash.
My eyes lit up when his fine ass walked up on stage. Kash was dressed in all white like me. He wore white jeans, a white shirt, white sneakers, and a white LA hat. The iced out bling on his neck, wrist, and ears lit the entire backyard up. I didn't even warn Lori as I made my way across the backyard and to the front of the crowd, not giving two fucks who was mad. I wanted him to notice me.

"Bitch." Lori spat in my ear a few minutes later. She had made her way to where I was. The DJ gave Kash the microphone and when his deep baritone spoke, my pussy flipped cartwheels. It was a damn shame how a man could be so fine.
"Aye, I wanna thank y'all for coming out. I know a lot of you really fuck with my family. I know a lot of you here on some genuine shit. If you know me, you know my big sister is my everything. She's like a second mom to me. My sister more G and got more heart than a lot of you niggas."
People nodded their heads in agreement and clapped.
"Why because she took a case?" I turned and looked at the dude next to me, and before I could even blink, security dragged him out of the party.

"Aye, Cuz. Don't let that nigga leave until I get to him." Kash said. Chills ran down my spine when his eyes landed on me. He then looked back at the crowd.

"I know it's a bunch of OPPS in here pretending they fuck with us. Warning. Don't let us find out who you are. Now, y'all muthafuckas give it up for my fine ass boss ass sister Chasity "Cali Gurl" Bryant!"

"Damn." Lori blurted. *Double damn,* I thought when she walked on the stage. Here I was picturing a stud looking chick, but his sister was gorgeous. When I say she was running neck and neck with Megan Thee Stallion, I was being 100. From her body to her facial features, she was stunning. She wore a red wine colored curve clenching Versace body dress with a pair of black red-bottom six-inch Christian Louboutin pumps. The breathtaking platinum tennis bracelet adorned her left wrist with a matching diamond necklace. The crowd cheered and everyone who wasn't already standing, stood to their feet. The crowd clapped and cheered when she hugged Kash. The close bond between the two could be felt. I hoped she wasn't one of those bitches who be all in her brother's business.

Tokyo

I chilled under the shade tree in my mom's backyard. While everyone was enjoying the festivities that occurred at my momma's BBQ, my mind was on seeking revenge. It had been three days since I attended the party Kash threw for his sister, and three days since I heard from Jersey and Aaliyah's stupid ass. I was pissed. When I got pissed, nothing good came from it.
"Girl, you been sitting over here quiet all day. What's your problem?" My cousin Mona asked. While she took it upon herself to cop a seat in the empty chair next to me, I continued to stare at the kids dancing down a soul train line.

"Ko-Ko, you hear me talking to you." She snapped. Ko-Ko was my childhood name. Only my family could address me as such.

"I ain't got no problem. Just chilling. I'm good." I answered.

"Bitch, I know you. Spill the tea."

Mona was my big cousin. We were four years apart. She was a ghetto superstar. She had four kids and four different baby daddies. Mona and I were on different levels, but I loved and trusted her.

I took off my oversized designer shades and held them in my hand. I looked at my big cousin. Between her and my momma, I could always keep it buck. We didn't talk on a daily basis, but she had my back, regardless.

"So, I went to this party the other day. I got embarrassed. Long story short, I got drunk and high and ended up doing some shit I ain't had no business. On top of that, I ain't heard from Jersey." I confessed.

She pursed her lips before taking a gulp from the red cup she was drinking from. As bad as I needed a drink, I was cool. I over did it at the party.

"I heard you went to Kash's party. Let the boy nut all over your face. I assumed you were high and drunk. That should tell you, it ain't what you do, but how you do it. Know your limit. I'm going to check your friend when I see her. She shouldn't even have let you get like that. It's over now. No need to dwell on it."

My mouth was dry from being open. After I was over the shock, I took the cup from her hand.
"How the hell you know, and when were you going to tell me?" I took a gulp from the cup, waiting on her to explain.

"Bitch, it's on the Hood News' page. You can't see his face, though. The bust-down with the KB on it everyone knows it's him." She shook her head. "That nigga walking around with my salary on his neck. Damn."

Hood News was a page on IG that posted all the drama around the city. I was going to be sick.
"Bitch, it'll blow over. If you feel some kind of way say the nigga raped you and get paid."
I blinked a few times. I knew she was trying to help but that was going too far. Shaking my head, I concluded this was all Jersey's fault. If he would've broken up with Aaliyah then I would've been with him and none of this would've happened.
"And, you still letting lame ass Jersey play you? He ain't leaving your sister, girl." She stood up. "You're too pretty and talented for the shit you're doing. I ain't trying to be funny, but never mind."

She walked off. Mona stopped in mid-stride and looked at me. "I love you. You are the shit. Act like it." She said sincerely.

Mona's words played in my head the entire ride from my momma's house. She was right. I am the shit. Being that I'm the shit, I deserved everything I wanted plus more. I was no longer going to let Jersey string me along.

Aaliyah

The last four days with my man had been the best. Every second, Jersey was doing stuff that reminded me of why I fell in love with him. The great sex, the room service, the walks on the beach and shopping sprees. I couldn't be happier. Although I had too much to do as far as school and tutoring, I dreaded ending our baecation. It was so refreshing to get away.

After we left the hotel, Jersey decided that we would go grab a bite to eat. I was down with that. I loved to eat good food.
While Jersey was talking business on the phone, I was on my iPad checking emails. When I saw that my mother emailed me, I immediately turned my phone back on and called her.

"Hey, Mommy." I said the moment I heard her sweet voice.
"I was worried. You nor Tokyo were answering."
"I'm sorry. I'm on a little vacay with Jersey. I turned my phone off so we could have alone time. I'm okay, though."

I frowned as my mom let out a hard dry cough. It sounded as if she would cough up a lung.

"Ma, get some water." She kept coughing. Now I was becoming nervous.

"I'm okay, baby. I think I'm getting a cold. Did you read the email that I sent?"

"No. When I saw it was you, I called." I went to the email on my iPad and read it. My mom was informing me that my father's lawyer was trying to reach out.

"She has my number." I said confused.

"No, that's the son. Frances passed away a few months ago. She died in her sleep of a massive heart attack. She was only 54 years old. So sad."

"Oh, wow! I hate to hear that." Frances had been around since I was a kid. It was sad to learn of her passing. I wished we could've gone to her funeral. My mother and I both loved her.

"Me too. She was such a good person."
I agreed.
"Are you still with your boyfriend?" She asked, changing subjects. My mom hardly ever referred to Jersey by his name. She didn't like him. Mainly because I said he was a dope boy, and she didn't think he was good enough for me. She always said he seemed like a snake.

"Yes, Mommy."
"Well, when you are alone, reach out to him. He has a surprise for you." She was referring to my dad's lawyer.

I wanted to ask if she knew what it was. The only time Daddy's lawyer reached out was when they had a monetary gift that he wanted me to have. I kept my comment to myself. My momma would flip if she knew Jersey was in my financial business.

We pulled into the restaurant's parking lot and both Jersey and I finished our calls.
The valet opened both of our doors, and we got out. My stomach growled when I smelled the food.

Hand in hand, Jersey and I walked into the restaurant. Immediately, a polite waitress greeted us and took our reservation. As the waiter escorted us to our seats, butterflies replaced the hunger pain. Jersey had me all giddy inside. Bypassing a large party, I couldn't help but frown on how loud they were. We were at an upscale restaurant. The group cursed and someone even said the word *nigga.*

When Jersey stopped in mid-stride, I watched as he walked up to the table. He was standing there for a few seconds with his hand out. I looked at the person he was in front of and was shocked. I tutored Mr. Bryant and couldn't believe it was him. He looked at Jersey as if he was from Mars.

Jersey finally put his hand down. I heard a few giggles. That was so damn rude. I knew my man, and he tried hard to mask his annoyance, or should I say embarrassment.

"KB, this my girl Aaliyah. Baby, this is KB." Jersey introduced us to each other.

KB looked at Jersey and smirked. He then looked at me. With a big grin, he spoke.

"What's up, Miss Aaliyah? We still on for Tuesday?" I felt guilty from the way he said it. It didn't help when he lustfully gave me the once over. Our connection was innocent, but I swear he didn't make it seem that way.

I could feel Jersey staring at me.

"Yes, of course." I replied. After all, he was my client.

With that, I turned to the greeter who was acting as if she wasn't in our business. We made eye contact, she offered a pleasant smile, and headed towards where she would seat us. I heard Jersey say his goodbyes.

Once we sat down, the waitress walked right off. I looked at Jersey and the veins were popping from his neck. His facial scowl made me uneasy. The palms of my hands began to sweat and my heartbeat sped up.

"What the fuck that nigga talking about?" He asked through tight teeth.

I was taken aback, Jersey had never snapped at me or seemed so angry with me.

"I tutor Mr. Bryant. He goes to my school."

"How the fuck is that, and he sells more dope than me? That's my supplier." Jersey snapped. He shocked the hell out of me. My client was a popular football player who had scouts looking at him. There was no way he could be a dope boy. Jersey's statement threw me for a loop. Even more so how Jersey talking illegal dealings in public? Even I knew that was a no no.

I looked around to see if anyone seemed like they were listening or watching us. When I glanced behind me, Mr. Bryant looked our way. I quickly turned my head.

"What you looking back at him for?" Jersey snapped.

"Baby, you are tripping. I don't want that man. I'm not a hoe. I don't cheat. I'm loyal and you know that."

"Yeah, whatever." Jersey was really tripping. I stood up.

"I'm ready to go. I ain't hungry."

Without saying a word, he stood and headed out of the restaurant leaving me behind. It was so obvious we had drama. At first, I did not look Mr. Bryant's way. When he said good-bye to me, I waved back.

"Say bye to my fine ass tutor, y'all." His behind was in trouble with me.

Aaliyah

"That was so gotdamn rude and embarrassing." I snapped the moment we got in the car. He glared at me before dismissing me by cutting his eyes at me and pulling off from the restaurant. I watched as he controlled the volume on the radio, on his steering wheel until it was blaring throughout the ride. Assuming that was his way of drowning me out, I crossed my arms over my chest and sat back in the seat. I was fuming. He tried to act like I was some scandalous bitch. Like I had anything to do with how the next muthafucka looked at me. Just like I didn't believe Jersey would cheat on me, he should've known damn well I wouldn't cheat on him. I wasn't even like that. I had only been sexually involved with three men in my entire life. Jersey knew that wasn't my character to be on no snake shit. Out of the two years we've been together, this was the first time he hurt my feelings.

Tears poured down my face and my leg shook uncontrollably. I fucking loved his ass. I would do anything for him, and he thought so small of me. I was in a zone, as Jersey sped down the highway like an idiot. He knew I didn't like it when he drove fast. The accident I had as a kid left me with PTSD, but since he was in his feelings, he didn't give a damn. He showed me how he really felt.

It wasn't long before we pulled into a gas station a few blocks from my house. Jersey didn't even bother to kill the engine. He bounced out of the truck, slamming the door behind him. I watched as he looked back at the pump before heading inside the gas station. He was straight tripping. I couldn't believe it. As much as I wanted to say something about his jealous rage, I refused. I hadn't done shit. So, if he wanted to act like that, then fine. I was still in my feelings, but he wasn't going to know.

To occupy my mind, I decided to go through the many texts I had since my phone was off over the weekend. I avoided everyone including my mother just to spend quality time with him. Ironically, I saw a text from Mr. Bryant. I rolled my eyes. I couldn't wait until Tuesday. I was going to give him a piece of my mind. I couldn't believe he was showing his ass like that. I shook my head with a smirk. He was so cocky and annoying, but that shit turned me on.

Time had passed, and I noticed Jersey hadn't gotten back in the car. I looked to see if he was pumping gas, but he wasn't. When my eyes scanned towards the gas station entrance, my heart rate increased. I couldn't get out the seatbelt fast enough. There were four dudes up on Jersey and one had a gun in his hand.

Once out of the car, I took off running towards him.

"Aye, get back before I call the police!" I yelled.

"Baby, get back in the car. And, you ain't calling the police." Jersey said to me. I looked at the dudes and one pointed his gun at me. I wished I had mine. I was far from one of those gangsta chicks, but I would shoot without hesitation if I felt me or someone I loved was in danger. I threw my hands in the air. I just knew he would shoot me. I could've pissed my pants.

"The shit you just said gonna get you killed. Bitch, do you know who you threatening?"

"Man, she's a good girl. She doesn't know about the street code." Jersey explained.

It happened so fast, I didn't see it coming.

Wham! The dude with the gun hit Jersey across the head. Blood immediately gushed from his head and trickled down his face. He stumbled a little but caught himself. I screamed, ran to him, and wrapped my arms around him.

"Please leave him alone. He ain't did nothing to you." I was in tears. The mess that was going on in front of me, I only saw on T.V. It was scary. I just knew they were about to kill him. The one with the gun spoke.

"Jersey, you better have my money like yesterday. It ain't hard to find you. Next time I'm killing you, and that's on gang." He gawked

before he walked away. His three flunkies followed.
Jersey and I were still standing in the same spot when they pulled up on us in a dark blue Maserati. Me and the driver, who was the gunman, made eye contact.
"You're too fine to be fucking with a lame ass nigga. If I were you, I would leave that fuck nigga where he at." He shook his head and pulled off. I let out a deep breath.

"Baby, you ok?"
Jersey snatched away from me.
"I'm good. Come on." Blood leaked down the side of his head.
When we got in the car, he pulled off. I reached up and turned the music down.
"What was that all about?" I asked.
"You heard the nigga. I owe him." He spat bitterly.
"How much?"
I was certain that it was street shit, so I didn't bother to ask why. Jersey looked from the road at me and then back at the road. "How much?" I wanted to know. I assumed it had to be a lot for his life to be threatened. Jersey gazed into my eyes.
"One hundred thousand." He looked back at the road. I was in total shock. How in the hell did he owe someone one hundred thousand dollars? I was speechless.
"Don't worry I got it." He said. I knew he was lying. Jersey had money, but I highly doubted he had that much.

When we pulled up to my house, I looked at my man.
"You need a hospital." I expressed out of concern.
"I'm good. Just go in the house. I'll hit you later." I couldn't believe he was leaving me home alone.
After grabbing my things, I stood in the driveway in total disbelief as he pulled off. What started as a day to remember turned out to be a day I wanted to forget.
I went inside. I was happy to have the house alone. I didn't feel like being bothered by anyone. I had taken a shower before we left the hotel, but I needed a hot bath. I went straight to my room and put

my things away. After running warm bath water, I lit a few candles and went back downstairs to get a glass of wine.

"This don't make no damn sense." I growled. The sight of the kitchen was disgusting. Tokyo had dirty dishes, a trashcan almost spilling over, and another trash bag next to it sitting right next to the refrigerator. Looking at her, you wouldn't even think she was nasty. She stayed fly and her car stayed shining. Nevertheless, she was filthy. I really felt like she didn't pick up behind herself because she knew that I hated a nasty house. I wasn't cleaning the shit up. I was gone for four days. I didn't dirty the place up. She could do that shit. Tokyo was a grown-ass woman. That's one reason why I was hesitant about letting her move in with me.

When I turned 18 years old, the lawyer popped up and gave me a birthday card and a letter. Letting me know that my dad left me and Tokyo the house. Since I was the first to officially become an adult, I was able to move in. Tokyo wasted no time moving in with me.

We lived in a small mini mansion out in Altadena. We had been living here for a good while. I loved our home, but I really was ready to move out with just my man. Atlanta couldn't come fast enough. Right after graduation, I was gone.

I headed to the cabinet where we kept the wine. It had been an adventurous and stressful day. All I wanted was Stella and Calgon to do its job and take me away.

Jersey

"Fuck!" I yelled the moment I pulled off from Aaliyah's. I wasn't even tripping off my fucking pounding ass head or the blood leaking down my face. I was pissed because the nigga found me, and out of all places, Altadena. Altadena was mostly uppity whites and blacks. You had to have money to be out there. Buddha was from the hood like me. Therefore, what was he doing out my girl's way? Was he following me? I had to get this nigga Buddha his money.

Summer of 2015

Buddha got at me and my homie Jam about running a play. He said there were some out-of-town niggas in the city, and they wanted to do business. They were transferring money from dormant accounts and needed people to go in and withdraw. After Buddha was paid, me and the homie were walking away with fifteen racks a piece. It was nothing to gathering up homies from the hood. The hood was always down to make money. Within a month, I made one hundred thousand alone. It was better than selling dope. Buddha ended up going to jail. Jam said he was cool on the plays. He didn't trust the niggas. He claimed they gave him FED vibes. I still wanted to run that shit and was low-key happy they got out the way. More money for me. I copped a whip, paid my bills up for a year, and got hell of fly shoes and clothes. Life was good. Then out of nowhere, I hadn't heard from the Denver niggas no-more. I started feeling like Jam, thinking they may have been the FEDS. That feeling changed when a month later I got a call from Buddha saying I owed him 60k.

"Nigga, how?" I wanted to know.

"Nigga, you was still doing business with my people. You thought they wasn't going to put me up on game? I'm the reason they ain't fucking with your sneaky ass no more. Take my money to my mom's crib." He hung up. I looked at my phone, wishing the nigga could see my face. He sounded stupid. Fuck I look like giving him 60k? I spent that shit and plus Cuz had like seven years in the joint. I made up my mind to deal with the shit when the time came and here it was. I guess he didn't do the seven year bid. Cuz was out early.

Buddha had a lot of pull in the city, and plus he was crazy. When my girl asked me how much I owed, I lied and told her 100k. I had good reasons. I knew she had the money and would give it to me. Aaliyah loved the fuck out of me. After she gave me the 100k, I was going to take 40k of it and flip it and, of course, it was for us.

I loved my girl with everything in me. I was just a fuck up. I was feeling some kind of way when Kash looked at her like he wanted to fuck. Plus, he tried to diss me acting like he didn't fuck with me. Instead of just saying Aaliyah was the tutor, the nigga was trying to make it sound like it was more than what it was. It wasn't Aaliyah I was mad at. I knew she wouldn't cheat on me. However, I wanted her to cut all ties with him. If she ever found out about all of my fuck ups, I wouldn't be able to take it if he were one of the niggas she ran to. I saw how he was looking at her. My bitch was fine, thick, smart, and loyal. I wasn't trying to lose her. My sour mood was no fault of Aaliyah's. It was the bitch Tokyo's fault and my own.

I pulled up to my crib. Between the hit in the head and seeing Tokyo's car in the driveway, my blood pressure felt like it rose a few notches. Ignoring the pounding from my head and shaky hands, I pulled off the Ralph Lauren polo I wore and wiped the side of my face. Tokyo stood by her car looking my way with a frown on her face. I couldn't help but notice how her body was banging in the bodysuit she wore. Tokyo was fine as fuck, but the bitch had an evil soul.

On the way from the hotel, I planned to finish enjoying my time with my girl, but I got a text from Tokyo with a paper showing that she was in fact pregnant, and we needed to talk ASAP. Fucked my mood all the way up. I didn't have no one to blame but myself. Holding the shirt to my head, I hopped out of my ride and made my way over towards the house. I lived right in the heart of the ghetto. It was a two-bedroom single family home. Before I remodeled the house a few years ago, it looked like a piece of shit like most of the houses on my block. The hood was just that, the hood, but it was home. I had been living there since birth. Everybody knew where I laid my head, including Buddha. I had to be extra careful.

As I made my way to the house, I watched my back to make sure no one was about to run up on me.

"Oh, my God! What happened to your head? Babe, you are bleeding everywhere." Tokyo said in a panic. She tried to reach for my head, but I moved out of the way.

"You wanted to talk. Let's go talk." I said, climbing the stairs. Once I unlocked the door, I allowed Tokyo to go in first, then me.

"Jersey, what in the hell happened to you? I'm no doctor, but you need stitches." I tossed the shirt on the floor. Eyeing the bottle of Remy I left on the table, I went and grabbed the bottle.

Tokyo

It was now day four and Jersey was still out with Aaliyah. I had been texting and cussing his ass out since yesterday. How in the fuck did he think it was cool to go lay up with that bitch for days, and here I was, sick and pregnant. Well, that's what I told him. Since I was his baby's momma, he should have been checking on me. My momma's good friend had come through with the positive pregnancy verification, and now I was about to give him a deadline to choose me or else. Yeah, Aaliyah's my sister and I should feel bad about wanting to be with her man, but she did me first. Although it was years ago, and I told her I forgave her, I still owed her.

To be perfectly honest, I did have feelings for Jersey. He wasn't paid like I preferred, but he was a hustler and when we weren't arguing over when he was leaving Aaliyah, we vibed good and had good sex. Bomb ass, nasty sex. The day he and Aaliyah left, I really wasn't tripping. Just like over a hundred times in the past, I was planning to leave Jersey's ass alone. I planned on snagging Kash and with Kash's rich ass, I would live happily ever after. However, that nigga tried me too, and soon I would have something for his ass even if it were ten years from now. No way was I going to let him get away with how he did me, and to make matters worse, it was all over the internet. I prayed Jersey didn't see the shit because he would trip hard. That nigga hated to think I was giving this good pussy away. That's what he constantly said.

Sitting in Jersey's yard waiting for him to pull up, so we could talk about this baby, I daydreamed about the first time we started messing around.

I year ago....

Being a hot fashion designer, I'm invited to a lot of parties and events. The Instagram icon Super Jet threw this particular party. The bitch did porn and fucked niggas for money since she was 16. Now at 25, she was a high demand. Her pussy got her rich. I knew some ballers were going to be at her party, that's why I told my girls we were going. It was me, Lori, and Taz. The theme was T-shirt, panties, and heels for the women and bare chest, shorts, and sneakers for the men. She held the event at a popular hall in Westchester. The bitch brought out the entire city, plus some. When I say there wasn't nothing but ballers and fine niggas in the building that is what the fuck I meant. Everything was free. The cocaine, pills, weed, meth, and the drinks were available at no charge to the party attenders. The only thing that we had to pay for was VIP. Therefore, I didn't pay but she was charging three hundred dollars to enter the rooms.

There were at least twelve rooms with an eight-person maximum. At first, I was just mingling, dancing and chilling. Once I got high and drunk it was a wrap for me. Taz roamed her hot ass off, and me and Lori decided to go be nosey together. We had checked out a few rooms, but we didn't want to join any. That was, until I felt someone come behind me and wrap their arms around my waist. I could smell the liquor on his breath. I was so high; I closed my eyes and giggled. Then I heard his deep voice.

"Did they tell you the rules before you came?" A funny sensation entered my body. I turned, looking into the eyes of Jersey. I knew the rules he was talking about, but I wanted to have a little fun with him.

"No, what are the rules? Would my sister's man like to tell me?" I smirked.

"When we're here, no names. The only connection is my dick going into every hole you got." He then looked at Taz. She walked up. Lori left. "Y'all join me and my boys."

Jersey entered a room not too far from where we stood. I looked at Taz and she looked at me. I shrugged, and we both followed. When I walked in, I saw Jersey getting head by a well-known underground fighter who went by the name Mr. Macho. That shit threw me for a loop. I stood there sipping my drink watching that hood ass nigga get head from another man. It was like an out of body experience. I undressed and made my way to where they were. The other two dudes in the room had a bitch occupied. She sucked dick while being fucked in the ass. I climbed on the bed and over Jersey's face. He wasted no time devouring my pussy. He ate my shit until I squirted in his mouth. Some kind of way, I ended up on my back. I looked to my left and Taz was being fucked by the nigga who had been giving Jersey head.

"Damn, you fine." I welcomed his meaty tongue in my mouth when he leaned down to kiss me.

"Oh, shit." I let out. Jersey had a muthafucking anaconda. I could take some dick, but it took me a minute to adjust to his shit. We all fucked from the night until the morning, with a few breaks to get high and drink in between. That was my first Super Jet party, but it wasn't the last.

The party wasn't Lori's thing but me and Taz were in those bitches every time she threw one. Each time I looked for Jersey to help me enjoy myself. I wasn't into gay shit, but it was something about Jersey getting head from another man that turned me on. Jersey and I both played by the rules. We never spoke about what we had going on. In fact, when we saw each other at the house we acted like we always acted, barely tolerating the other. I started to fantasize about Jersey on a regular. I eventually got jealous of him and Aaliyah. She didn't even know the real him, but was forever talking about her man this, her man that. I bet he never shared his secret with Aaliyah because her goodie two shoes ass would act as if he had committed a deadly sin.

One day, I was about to take a hot bath and forgot to get my drink. Butt naked, I ran to the kitchen and right into Jersey.

"Perfect timing." He said, licking his lips while taking me all in. He dropped the duffle bag that was in his hand.

"I just want a quickie. Is that cool?" The nigga didn't even have to ask. I turned around, grabbed my ankles and popped my ass. When that nigga entered me, it was heaven. That was the start of us fucking whenever Aaliyah wasn't around. A year and two months later, I was ready for us to be a full-blown couple. Shit, I was having his baby.

The loud music coming from behind me interrupted my day-dreaming. I already knew it was him. No one else would be coming in his driveway. His drunk ass daddy rode a bike. Attitude turned all the way up, I jumped out of my ride and stood by my door waiting for him. I was about to chew him a new asshole. Either he does right by me, or no one would be happy. I stood there watching him as he climbed out of his ride. He held the shirt he was supposed to have on against his face. Jersey was a few feet away from me when he took the shirt from his face. My eyes bucked when I noticed the bloodstains on it.

"What happened to you?" I reached for him, but he dodged me and kept walking. I was on his heels as he climbed onto the porch. Jersey opened the door and allowed me to walk in. When he shut the door, I looked at him as he made his way towards his coffee table.

"Jersey, what in the hell happened to you? I'm no doctor but you need stiches." Ignoring me, he tossed the shirt on the floor and grabbed the bottle of Remy that was on the table. Taking the top off, he took a gulp.

"I don't need no stitches. I need a pain pill, some coke, and some pussy from my fake ass baby's momma." Is what he said. I wanted to cuss his ass out. What the fuck he mean I was his fake ass baby's momma? However, since he was hurt I didn't say a word. Leaving out of the living room, I made my way to his bathroom. I found the pain pills inside the medicine cabinet. I took the entire bottle. The way his head was looking, he needed it.

After giving Jersey the pills, I decided to run him a shower.

"I ran you a shower, go get in." I sat on the couch.

"You are coming with me." With that, he walked towards the bathroom and of course, I followed. I couldn't wait to find out what happened to him.

A Few Days Later… Kash

The sun brightly shined on a Tuesday morning. A nice cool breeze hit me in the face. California was known for its perfect weather, constant sunshine, and chilled-out locales. I loved Cali and everything about it. L.A. was overcrowded, traffic was a bitch, the Mexicans outnumbered every race in the city, and the police were always fucking with a minority. But, nevertheless, I loved my city. Folks were leaving the city because of the high cost of living and gang violence. I welcomed it. Born and raised at 19, I would forever call this place home.

Dipping in and out of traffic in my red Dodge Challenger, seat leaned back and Nipsey Hussle's mixtape titled Crenshaw blared through the speakers, I was in a zone. I had an eventful weekend that seemed to go by too damn fast. I smiled, thinking about how my sister was home. I was happier than a mofo. Chasity was sent to prison for being the driver of a getaway car. She helped her nigga commit a robbery. They were out in Beverly Hills having lunch when the nigga ran into someone who owed him. Old boy didn't have what he owed, so Von took his watch and chain. He probably would've gotten away with it if dude wasn't with his white aunt, who just so happened to be DA. In a matter of minutes, the police had them surrounded. Von jumped out and ran. Eventually, he was caught. I guess the DA was just that pissed, she took my sister down too. They tried to give her seven years, but our lawyer saved her. 'Chas' did sixteen months and had to do a year on probation. I was happy she was home. My sister was like my second momma but the home girl at the same time. She did everything for me. Literally, she was my best friend. I couldn't wait to give her a surprise on her birthday. My second favorite part about the weekend was seeing Aaliyah.

Pulling into the lot of SC, my school, I picked up my energy drink

from the cup holder and took a few gulps until it was gone. I had three classes today. I wasn't ready. Like I said, my weekend was turned up, but school was an important part of my life. I couldn't fuck that off. No matter how much I made on the side assisting my father with his drug game.
I parked. The clock on my dash read 7:45am. I had about eighteen minutes to get to class.

"Hey, Kash. I can't wait until your game." Some chick called out as I was passing her through the hall.
"Thanks." I countered.
Later On That Day
I'd just walked out of my last class for the day. I stopped and talked to a few folks before making my way to my car. I had an hour before my tutoring session with Ms. Aaliyah. If I was late, I knew that was my ass.

Being a star athlete had its benefits. I had a permit to park close to each building I had a class in. On days like this one, when a nigga was hungry and tired, I appreciated my superstar treatment.
The moment I got in the car and pulled off my phone rung.
Whoever it was knew I didn't fuck with No-Caller ID calls. I pressed ignore and turned my music all the way up. I stopped at Fatburger and headed back to campus to enjoy my food. That was short lived when my ex-Darla called.
"What, man?" I answered, annoyed. "You claimed you needed time and space. You said you was cool on a nigga, but you won't stop calling."

"I'm glad I left your ass. How embarrassing of you to be screwing all over the net. Posting pictures like it's cute."

"I wasn't fucking nobody. I got my dick sucked. Now mind yo gotdamn business!" I yelled and hung up on her, bipolar want to be my momma and not my girlfriend ass. Darla and I had been rocking for two and a half years. I gave her whatever she wanted and treated her like a queen. No, a nigga wasn't walking a straight line, but what I did never got back to her. Darla was a spoiled rich kid who looked down on my friends and where I come from. She let her momma and her lonely ass sister pump her head up about me over the time of our relationship. She was always telling me what they said. That shit went in one ear and out of the other. People were telling me she was jealous of the bond I had with the folks I held dear to me, like my sister. All of a sudden, when she knew my sister was coming home and all the shit, I had planned for her, she wanted to give the relationship a break. I didn't like that jealous, spoiled shit. Once we break up ain't no coming back.

I thought about the video that was going around of me letting that fashion designer hoe top me off. I was fucked up. I wasn't even the type of nigga that slung my dick to this bitch and that bitch. Especially a hoe I didn't know. On me, I think someone spiked my drink. On the other hand, I could've been just that fucked up.

For the first time ever, I made it to my tutoring session before Ms. Aaliyah. I had my book, note pad, and pens out. I just received a text from my sister when I looked up and Aaliyah was walking towards me. Looking at Aaliyah's fine ass strutting my way, all I could think about was how Darla fucked up and so did Aaliyah's punk ass nigga. Aaliyah was going to be mine. I didn't expect to see her with Jersey's clown ass at the restaurant. I didn't take her for a chick that dated lames. What put the icing on the cake was I knew the nigga was fucking her sister. The hoes that rolled up on her that day weren't lying. I overheard a few homies talk about how Jersey was banging his girl's fine ass sister. I had no idea that Jersey was messing with my girl. Yeah, I was claiming her. I ain't no saint, but I'd never have my girl looking stupid like that. Her sister, that was cold.

Juicy, that is the nickname she didn't know I had given her. She wore a floral print sleeveless maxi dress with a thigh-high side slit that gliding over her curves. Her hair was worn in a short style with tight curls. If she knew how many times, I fantasized about

wrapping my fingers in her hair and fucking her, she'd slap me or hop on my dick.
My baby was a few feet away. I smiled and she grinned back. I scooted her chair back, and she took a seat. I went and sat back down across from her.
"You look nice." I complimented.

"Thanks, Mr. Bryant. So do you." She replied, all chipper and shit. Aaliyah may have acted like she didn't like me, but I knew for now she was feeling a nigga even if it was just my style.

"So, how's school?" She asked, digging in her book bag. She placed all of the items she needed on the desk.

"Thanks to my juicy ass tutor, a nigga ain't getting no less than a B on all his tests. You know your boy smart. It's just that history ain't for me, but you made the shit easy." I reached across the table and grabbed her hand. Looking into her eyes, I spoke. "Let me take you out to thank you. Pleeeassse." I hit her with the one dimple smile.

I knew what the fuck I was doing. Chicks were already drawn to a nigga because your boy is handsome, talented, and my swag is like none of the others. However, my Colgate smile drives them crazy. The way Aaliyah stared at me before gently removing her hand, confirmed what I already knew. She was digging me, but that lame had her heart.
"You so damn pretty to me."

"Mr. Bryant. Please stop." It was the way she said it though.

Aaliyah

"Hey, baby girl. What are you doing?" My mom asked when I answered the phone.

"I'm in the restroom. Just finished my tutoring session. I'm thinking about calling Val to go out with me for happy hour." After washing my hands, I looked myself over in the library's small restroom mirror. Being around Kash was making me feel weird. Like, nervous and shy. I felt bad for thinking it, but I really was trying to see what it was that Kash saw in me. Not that I was interested in him or anything. It was just that I was curious. I may be on the thick side, but I was solid. My butt was real, and so were my boobs. My stomach wasn't all that flat, but I hid it well. I was always complimented on my blemish free caramel colored complexion. In my opinion my honey-colored eyes, long lashes, and full lips were my best features. Like I said, I'm pretty, but I didn't think the type of pretty that would have a person like Kash checking for me. I knew he had a woman or women, I wasn't crazy.

"Le-Le, are you there?" My mother's sweet voice pulled me from my trance.

"Yes."

"So, have you?"

"Have I what?" I asked, walking out the restroom. I stood in the hallway to finish our conversation.

"Have you called the lawyer?"

"No. I will soon." I wanted to tell her I had a lot on my mind, and I totally forgot, thanks to Jersey and how he had been acting, but I kept it to myself. She already didn't like him.

"Mom, I will call you tonight. Okay?"

"Okay, I love you." She coughed. She had been doing a lot of that lately. I made a mental note to talk to her about that.

"You ready?" Kash asked. He was standing by the exit when I came from the restroom. I nodded my head yes. We walked to the car in silence. When I got to my car, I spoke.

"Kash." I said, calling him by his first name. The way he looked at me, I could tell he was shocked.

"I'm on first name basis now? What's up though, Juicy?" He smiled before biting his bottom lip. I shook my head.

"Who's Juicy?" I asked, faking an attitude.

"Only if you knew what I knew." He rubbed his hands together while looking over my body.
"Enlighten me." I put my hand on my hip.
See, this is why Jersey was tripping. Kash was a real-life ladies man, but I wouldn't be bitten by his fangs.

"You are going to be my woman."
My mouth dropped. After I was over the shock, I went in.

"Mr. Bryant, cut that out. You know I have a man. A man who just so happens to be your friend. I'm not like that."

"First off, that nigga ain't my friend. I don't know what he told you, Juicy. That's not my friend. I don't fuck with niggas like him." He shrugged.

Wow? I thought. What was he trying to say about my baby? He was so rude and cocky. This man was something else.

"Well, he said you were his supplier. Shouldn't the people you associate with be considered friends?" I frowned. "I'm not trying to be in your business. But, sweetheart." I paused for a brief moment. "Kash, you have an entire future ahead of you. Scouts are watching you. When you're on that field, you are so fucking good. A showoff, but a muthafucking beast. Football will take you so far without any risk of losing your freedom. Why are you risking your blessing? I know what my man does. I pray he walks away before it's too late. I also pray that you leave that shit alone before you lose what's really meant for you, and it ain't that life."

The scowl he wore let me know he didn't receive my message, and that saddened me. Thinking about how another young black man was risking everything for street fame was heartbreaking. However, when his face softened and that one dimple that I adored showed I let out a sigh of relief. He heard me.

"Thanks, Juicy. You give a fuck." He kissed me on the cheek. My stomach fluttered.

"I'll see you next week." He opened my car door and I got in.

"Oh, and to keep it buck, I ain't nobody's supplier. I don't know what dude running his dick suckers about." With that, he shut my door. For some odd reason, I wanted to make sure he was safe. So, I waited until he got in his car before I pulled off.

The moment I was on the highway, I called Jersey. Ever since the day he was hit with the gun, he had been acting funny. I knew he was stressed, and that's why I was trying to make life easier for him, but he wouldn't let me.

"Babe, let me call you back. I'm busy." Jersey said when he answered and before I could respond, he hung up. Yeah, I needed a drink. Happy hour sounded good. I called Val.

Val was my best friend. We had been girls since high school. She was the wild, confident, and outspoken one. I was more mellow and nonchalant but trust me I wasn't a push over, I just didn't like drama. Val and I were like night and day, but we wouldn't trade the other for anything. We used to kick it almost every day. Tokyo would complain that I acted like Val was my blood sister instead of her. When Val hooked up with her baby's daddy Tiger, we stopped kicking it as much. We may have seen each other once a month, if that. Once Val and I stopped kicking it as much, Tokyo hadn't tried to hang out with me not one time. My sister was so selfish at times, but that's my sister, so I had to deal with most of her shit.

Speaking of Tokyo, she has been acting very distant and stank. I didn't know what it was that she was going through. She always put on a front like everything was good with her. Which was stupid when it came to me. I was her sister, so I damn sure would not judge her. Her ass hadn't come home last night and when I called her, she declined my calls twice. If Jersey would've come over, I would have enjoyed the alone time, but he claimed he was working. Bored out of my mind, I grabbed a good book and read it until I went to sleep. I was so glad Val and I, would be hanging out later. I was going to get tipsy, go home, and crash since Jersey was working.

"So you mean to tell me he flipped out on you because another nigga was flirting with you?" I shared with my BFF how my man had been acting. We didn't keep secrets, but I would not tell her about the dude who pistol whooped him. That was street stuff.

"Yes, acted like I was a hoe. Like I have ever given him a reason to not trust me." I rolled my eyes, just thinking about how he acted had me pissed. I knew he was stressed, but he needed to apologize. I would give him some time.

The bartender brought my strawberry daiquiri and Val a triple shot of Hennessy. I knew my BFF, and something was bothering her, but I would give her time to tell me.

"Best friend, the nigga knows what he has and a snake hoe ain't it. The way you say he was acting can mean one or two things." She looked at me and then took her drink to the head, slamming it on the counter. "Good shit." She acknowledged. "Like I said, either one or two things could be the reason. Either he's insecure because he knows you deserve more than what he is offering, or the nigga doing something himself. Don't forget he was cheating on his girl with you."

I stared at her blankly. Jersey had never given me a reason to believe that he was cheating just as I never gave him a reason to think that I was cheating. Nevertheless, he had been acting strange now that I thought about it, maybe the signs had been there, and I just didn't want to see that. Because I loved Jersey and I knew that he loved me.

"I know you don't want to think like that, friend, but if you ain't trying to investigate, then wait. It'll fall in your face if he's cheating. To keep it buck, he ain't on your level." She shrugged. I didn't say anything. My stomach balled up in a knot. Was my nigga cheating on me?

I didn't want to seem bothered, so I waited a few minutes before I excused myself to the restroom. Luckily, it wasn't a wait. I walked in. The attendant who sold the sprays, chewing gum, lip-gloss and whatever a girl needed at the club spoke to me. I returned the greeting. Turning my back on her, I called Jersey. He didn't pick up. I sent him a few texts, and the shit was undeliverable. I swear to God, if he was cheating, I was going to knock the black off his ass and leave him the fuck alone. Muthafucka!

Pissed was an understatement. I stepped out of the bathroom, ready to have something stronger than the drink I ordered. I was also ready to tell my homegirl how she may have been right. Jersey probably was doing something he had no business doing. As I was walking down the hall, I bumped into a familiar face. I was prepared to apologize, but I froze when I looked up and right into his eyes.

Getting a good look at the mean ass man in front of me or should I say dangerous ass man that was in front of me, I couldn't help but take note of how handsome he was. Even with the deep frown on his face, I couldn't help but notice his attractive features.

Standing about 6'1 medium built with tattoos all over his arms and neck. His butterscotch complexion was blemish free. He had the perfect light brown bedroom eyes, cute long nose, and thick lips. It was such a shame how a man so handsome could be so dangerous.

After Mr. Dangerous looked at me from head to toe, he smirked before gently taking me by the wrist. I tensed up, but I knew better than to put on a scene. He whispered in my ear causing chills to run down my body. Yet again, I was caught slipping without my gun. I stood there and listened.

"I pressed your punk ass man at the gas station, and you threatening to call the police on me. I'ma let that slide, but don't ever in your life threaten to call the police on me or any hood nigga. We don't play that shit. I'm sure that lame that you fuck wit' didn't tell you that. Just like he didn't tell you that he fucked a good nigga out of a lot of bread. The nigga that he fucked out of the bread don't play."

"I did my research on you. I followed you to your school and found out who your father was and your sister. You're a good girl. You shouldn't be in his mix. Leave that punk ass nigga alone. If he doesn't pay his debt, everyone associated with him becomes a target."

When he let my arm go, I scurried off. What type of shit did Jersey get me into? When I made it back to the bar, Jersey's friend named Jam sat in my spot chatting with Val.

"Where's Jersey?" I asked, almost in a panic. I didn't know him like that. I only saw him a few times, but we were introduced, so he knew I was Jersey's girl.

"I haven't seen him in a couple of days. I thought he was with you. Then again." He paused. Staring at me like he wanted to say something more.

"Then again what?" I wanted to know. He shook his head. "Call him. I don't know."

I gave him a head nod. Val asked me if I was ok. I told her I was ready to leave. She gave me a head nod. I watched in shock as she handed Jam her phone. I figured he was giving her his number.

"I'm going to call you." She smiled.

Wow, Val and Jam trying to hook up, I thought to myself. The one who said she would never date outside her race. The one who said she would never leave Tiger and let another bitch get her bag was giving out her number to a white boy. Yeah, she and I both had shit going on.

Kash

You wildin' bro, I thought as I walked out the grocery store. I went in there to grab some chips, juice, and a Snickers bar. I didn't cook, but I knew how to make the hell of out breakfast food. Therefore, I picked up waffles, eggs, sausage, grits, and shit like that too.

Damn near the entire time in the store, thoughts of Aaliyah were on my mind. It had been a few days since I last saw her. The shit she said to me about my future and how she was rooting for me touched a nigga's mind, soul, and heart. I was already digging Juicy, but the sincerity behind her words had me feeling her that much more. It's true what they say, there's always somebody cheering for you, and a lot of times they are people who aren't in your circle. Her words not only touched me, but also had me thinking about the moves I was making. I wasn't getting my hands dirty but still, I was risking my freedom. I had to agree with what she said.

I hit the locks on my red Dodge Challenger and put the bags in the trunk. There was a white Honda Civic with the windows rolled down, allowing me to see two little kids inside. They probably were around the ages of seven and eight. Their momma knew damn well they weren't supposed to be in the car alone. I put my last bag in the trunk and headed to climb in my ride.

"Hey, Mister. You in the red car." I looked towards the Civic in the direction of the high squeaky voice. It was a little baldhead girl with very thin hair that was as short as a boy's was. A small one-centimeter ponytail was on the top of her head. She smiled displaying a top grill full of silver teeth. I stared at her, wondering if she was talking to me. What the fuck did the kid want? Then it hit me. She wanted money. Kids stayed begging these days.

"What?" I asked, looking around to see if the momma was coming.
"You see our momma in 'da' store?" Silver teeth asked. Another head popped out the window, now both Baldy and the little fat light-skinned girl hung damn near out the car.
"I don't know your momma." I retorted.
"You don't? Her name Apples. She's light skinned like my sister. She got a biggo booty like a horse." She smiled bigger than a rainbow. "She says she's slim thick."
"Nah, I don't know her. What's up?" I asked, wondering if it was something important. The yellow chubby one sitting beside her mean mugged me with her arms folded.
"I can't stand my momma." She rolled her eyes. At this point, I realized their little asses were just too gotdamn grown. "Every time she goes to the store, she buys her boyfriend all the good snacks and then buys us the little cheap ones from the dollar store. When his gone, he eats ours too. Ole greedy bastard."
Baldy added. "We should tell 'us' grandma, so she can call Section 8, and they put him out. I hate him." She pouted.
Even though their asses were grown ass fuck, I felt what they were saying. Their momma was trifling, and they knew it.

"Tink- Tink and Pooka! What have I told y'all bad asses about talking to strangers?" I looked to my left and noticed a chick wearing a pink bonnet, black pajama set, and pink house slippers. I assumed that was their momma. All I could do was shake my head, her ass looked a mess.

"Aye, Apples. You better buy those kids some good snacks, or I'm calling section 8. I got your license plate." With that, I slid in my car, shut the door, and turned my music up before pulling off. I was laughing my ass off.

I chilled at the pad for a few hours before I got a text from the homie Quan telling me to slide through. I told him I would, but first I wanted to slide up on this one chick. A nigga needed some pussy.

I walked in the spot about 11 o'clock at night. Our spot wasn't some little two-bedroom trap house with fucked up furniture and sheets for curtains. We didn't have dope heads running in and out. We called it a spot because that's where we talked business and chilled. Our shit was located in the Baldwin Hills area. The five bedroom that was owned by me and my sister was in a quiet middle- class neighborhood. When I walked in the door, Jam, Yogi, and Born were sitting in the living room. They all burst into laughter.

"What the fuck y'all niggas laughing at?" I asked with a frowned expression.

"Nigga, you burnt." Born, my right hand laughed. They were all giggling, looking at Jam's phone. I stood there wondering what the fuck was funny before I snatched the phone from Jam's hand.

"You a star, nigga. You know you can't be having shit like this leaked. USC will fuck around and kick you out." When they said that, I already knew what they were talking about. I looked at the phone and shook my head.

"So, the bitch didn't delete it." I said aloud to myself. I hit up Queen. She was the bitch that they said ran the Instagram page that the video and flick were posted on. I told her to take it down. She told me she was, so I guess she lied. I made a mental note to have the homegirls fuck her up.

"Nah, it's deleted, but it's still floating around." Jam said, shaking his head. I was annoyed about the shit, but it was out there, and there was nothing I could do about it.

"So, that's what you called me over here for?" I asked the homie.

"Nah." He sat up on the couch. Born looked at Jam.

"You tell him. It's your boy." Born said to Jam. I looked at Yogi because he was reaching for the bottle of Patron on the table.

"Let me hit that." I said. Yogi took a gulp and passed it to me.

"What you gotta tell me, Jam?" Jam was a white boy, the homie too. A lot of people underestimated him because he didn't grow up in the hood. However, some black people raised him, and so he knew how to adjust to the culture. His uncle was one of my father's bodyguards. The nigga Nark was a goon, and I think that's where Jam got it from. He was loyal to the soil. I trusted him just as much as I trusted the other niggas in front of me.

Jam started. "You know Buddha's out?" Buddha was my auntie's husband's son, so we called each other cousin. We didn't hang out, but when we saw each other it was love.

"Yeah, I heard. I been meaning to get up with him."

"Long story short, Jersey owes the nigga some money. I hear it's like sixty racks." Jam explained. "He and Buddha had some shit going on when he was out. When fam got locked up, Jersey ran off with his money. Word on the street is he pistol whooped the nigga Jersey a few days back. You know he's going to kill him if he don't pay." I nodded to agree. "Buddha don't give a fuck, but you know that."

Jam was right. Buddha was a no-nonsense type of nigga. I'm surprised he didn't kill Jersey's lame ass that day. I thought about Aaliyah and how she was connected to the nigga. She didn't even know her life was in danger. I found myself wanting to protect her. On the inside, I was hot thinking about her getting hurt. I never liked Jersey. He was Jam's boy. He made runs for him and with him. I knew a weak nigga when I saw one, and he was it, but we needed extra help to make drops. So, I allowed Jam to vouch for the nigga. Now that I knew he was a snake, he was off payroll and that was that.

"Fire the nigga." I said to Jam.

"Say less." He replied.

I sat back in deep thought thinking about calling Aaliyah just to hear her voice and to let her know a real one was thinking about her.

"Aye, Kash." Yogi called my name.

"What's up?"

"You know the bitch who face you bust in?"

"Yeah." He was referring to the Instagram fashion designer Tokyo.

"Did you know that she's Jersey's girl's sister?" I looked at the nigga

like he was crazy. I had to play it off. My heart was thumping like it was about to leap from my chest. *Nah,* I thought to myself.
I let the girl I wanted and wanted a future with sister top me off.
On top of that, she was the same sister who fucked her man.
I fucked up.
"Word." Was all I said and shook my head.

Tokyo

"So you know Sammamish fucking Steven, right? He's only sleeping with her because she let him keep his work at her house. You know that fine ass Mexican don't like her black crusty ass. Always wearing those ugly synthetic wigs. Anyway, girl, he slipped up and got her pregnant. She was all in the projects, claiming that he was leaving his girl for her. He wasn't going to leave a classy chick, for her ugly ratchet ass. Girl, she found out that he was marrying his girlfriend and the bitch showed up to the wedding reception."

It was close to 3 o'clock in the morning. I sat at the desk going over information with the bondsman to get Jersey released. We couldn't even focus on what we were doing because a bamboo earring wearing, five braids to the back hoe that needed to come out ASAP talked loud on the phone about somebody else's ghetto ass business. She wore a dingy white tank top with a pair of blue jean booty shorts.

"Girl, showed up at the reception. Girl, guess who she took with her? You ain't gon' believe who it was. It was Juju's thieving ass. I heard Sammamish was in there acting a fool. Belly flopped on the cake table and trying to destroy shit. Juju stole somebody's mink coat. Girl, the police caught their asses running down the street like they were about to get away. You know Sammamish's fat ass can't run. Girl, I fell out laughing when I heard that. HAHAHAH..." She cackled like a hen slapping her leg and all.

The bondsman tried to ignore her, but when I gave him an irritated look, he finally spoke up.

"Miss." The bondsman called out. "Can you lower your voice? This is a place of business." She looked at him like he was stupid.

"This is my business while you all up in mine." She stood up. "Let me go, there are plenty of bondmen around here." She stormed off, calling him a racist.

I took a deep breath and continued to finish the paperwork.

A few hours prior....

I spent the night with Jersey. We talked about the baby and us being together to raise our child as a family. He was honest with me and told me that he loved Aaliyah, and he didn't want to break her heart. He said he was trying to wait until she left for Atlanta before he broke the news, that way he wouldn't be in her face after she found out about the betrayal. Like, I told him, she slept with my man first, so it's her karma. I told him I wanted her to know ASAP or I would tell her myself. He begged me to give him a couple of months and I did. Around noon, we departed ways. He went to go handle his business and I went to the office to meet a few clients. I say around 2 o'clock Jersey text me and told me to meet him at the house because it was an emergency. When I pulled up, he was already there. Before I could even get out of the car, he was standing on the porch. The closer I got, I could see the scowl on his face. My heartbeat quickened, wondering what was wrong with my baby's daddy.

"What happened?" I asked when I stepped on the porch. I thought it had something to do with whomever hit him in the head. I couldn't even get the words out good enough. Wham! That nigga punched me in my head so hard I saw stars. I was too dizzy to swing back. Jersey grabbed me by the throat and snatched me in the house. When he tossed me on the floor, I hit my back hard. The pain was unbearable. He stood over me huffing and puffing. I then realized that he set me up and was trying to kill the baby he thought I was pregnant with.

"Help!" I screamed out. Jersey looked like a mad man. He reached down and punched me in the head, arms, and legs.

"You a scandalous ass bitch. That baby ain't mine. I should stomp your hoe ass out, bitch." He growled and spit on me. I'm thinking to myself, *It ain't no one baby, so get your crazy ass off me.* I'm glad I didn't say what I was thinking. His next words told everything.

"I saw you getting fucked on camera. You let that nigga nut in your face. You a slut, bitch. You could never be Aaliyah, you dirty hoe."

I squeezed my eyes shut and sobbed at his revelation. Now that I knew why he was beating my ass, it hurt more than the pain his punches caused. I was so embarrassed and hurt.

"You can't be my baby's momma. That ain't even my baby. You're a hoe." I shook my head no. I was crying so hard I couldn't even get the words out of my mouth.

"Freeze, police." I heard and when I opened my eyes there were several sheriffs in the house with guns drawn on Jersey. The look he gave me when he was cuffed told me what I knew he was thinking. He was disgusted with me, not only that, but he wanted no parts of our baby.

I sat at his house and called every hour until he made bail. The moment he made bail, I flew my ass downtown to get him out. I hoped me apologizing would help. I lied and blamed Kash and his friends for drugging me. I hoped that eventually he would forgive me. If not, I was going to have to do what I had to do. He wasn't leaving me and my child.

Val

Hanging out with my BFF for the first time in what felt like forever felt good. I missed her pretty smile, low-key vibe, but down for whatever her best friend wanted to get into. The night after we left the bar, we went back to her house. She voiced her concern about how she was seeing the signs that maybe Jersey was cheating on her and if he was, she was leaving his ass. I knew she loved him, and although I didn't want her heartbroken, I hoped she left his ass alone. Jersey was a lame. Being that I hung out with my dude a lot at the studio – no one knew, but I wrote Tiger's lyrics. I got an ear full about these niggas in the streets. It was true, niggas talked like bitches. I didn't have proof so, I wasn't about to take half ass information back to my BFF, but I heard Jersey was a down-low nigga. I also heard he was scary and never wanted to fight, but was quick to pull his gun. They said he was a snitch too. My dude and his friends said he turned his own cousin in, that's why he was so paranoid.

Speaking of my man, I shared with Le-Le how I was ready to leave my baby's daddy. Tiger was doing too much. His ass would stay coked up for days and sleep for weeks. Claiming he was stressed out. How? I was the one writing his music, setting up shows and events, and picking out his wardrobe. He didn't do shit but record, perform, and do drugs.

I flushed the toilet and walked over to the sink to wash my hands. Tonight Le-Le and I were going to a party that Jam invited me to. Jam is the white boy whose number I got the last time she and I went out. Le-Le really didn't do hood parties, but because I wanted to go, she said yes. I kind of thought she wanted to see if Jersey popped up. That nigga had been still MIA. However, per Jam he didn't mess with Jersey anymore. Therefore, I guess he wasn't going to be there, who knows.

Looking in the full-length mirror on the bathroom wall, I admired myself from top to bottom. I loved my milk chocolate complexion and straight white teeth. I stood 5'4 and weighed 185 pounds. It was in all the right places. The twenty grand I spent on my body was so worth it, and I wasn't ashamed to let a bitch know I went to the chop shop. My once flat ass was now plump and round. I've always had a flat stomach, but I still got lipo to make sure no fat was lingering around. I went from an A cup to a B cup. I got my teeth done and even lip injections. Therefore, my already dark chocolate ass went from an average looking chick with a body you'd frown upon to a sexy ass video vixen looking rapper's girlfriend. Tiger was making a name for himself in the industry. My BD was sexy and just like he said, I needed to match his sexiness. Therefore, I got the surgery. You'd think he would be jealous about how many niggas were on me, but nope, all he cared about were drugs and recording new music in the studio. He no longer showed me the love and affection he once did. It hurt, but I was so close to being fed up. Only if he knew.

Tonight I was rocking a pair of Versace leggings, a denim shirt that I tied in the front with a pair of heels. My hair was in a 36-inch weave. I was simple, but looked so damn good. When I walked out of the bathroom and into the bedroom, I shared with my baby's daddy, he was sitting on the bed holding the baby and staring at me. Our son was nine months old and the spitting image of his daddy but had my rich chocolate complexion.

"Where are you going looking like a hoe?" He asked, looking me up and down. That's another thing. Tiger was starting to be mad disrespectful and so was I.

"Your momma a hoe with her stank feet ass." I snapped. I went to kiss my baby on the cheek, so I could get the fuck away from this nigga, but Tiger pushed me away.

"I bet you won't tell my momma that in her face."

"I bet she won't wash her feet." I retorted. I tried to kiss my baby again, but he blocked me with his hand.

"You are such a childish dope head." I spat before grabbing my purse and walking out of the room. I wasn't worried about my baby being taken care of because his big ass momma lived with us and no matter how I felt about her old ass, she loved my son. Tiger was a momma's boy. The shit was annoying. The fat hoe blamed everything on me when we got into it, and never her trifling son.

"You look so cute, best friend." I said when Aaliyah climbed into my white Range Rover. Her hair was in a high ponytail with Chinese cut bangs. She wore a pair of lime green high- waisted shorts, a cropped top, and a pair of red bottom heels. She had a pair of cute bamboos in her ears, a gold watch and a custom necklace with her name on it.

"Thanks, girl." She looked towards the house and rolled her eyes.

Tokyo was on the porch, staring. I honked and waved, and she walked back inside. Tokyo was a bitch.

"What the hell is her problem?" I asked. We were now driving down the street.

"She's weird and always acting jealous. She had not said two words to me all day but as soon as she sees me dressed, she asked where I'm going. I knew she was mad when I told her, somewhere with you."

"Girl, fuck her bipolar ass."

"You heard from Jersey?" I asked. We were at a stoplight. I looked at my BF, and she stared out of the window.

"Nope. He came by because he left two duffle bags in my closet. I wouldn't have known he came by if I didn't see the bags."

"Nigga still leaving work at your house?" I asked, annoyed.

"I don't know what it is. It could be money."

"Nah, I bet its dope. But whatever." I felt Aaliyah looking at me. I felt like Jersey took her for granted.

I texted Jam letting him know we were close. He texted back, letting me know to pull in VIP, and he would be there waiting for us.

"Best friend, I think you are right. Jersey is on some other shit. If Jersey's up in here, we are setting this bitch off."

"I'm on whatever you on." I replied.

We stepped out of the car. Jam was looking good in his designers and sneakers. The blue hat that covered his braids going to the back set his swag off just right.

He spoke to Aaliyah, and then looked at me.

"Can I get a hug?" I knew the shit I was on could get me in trouble by Tiger, but I didn't care. I was tired of him and in need of some attention.

The club owner led us into the club without having to wait in line with the other patrons. Jam held our hands as he led us through a sea of people. Once we got to the entrance of VIP, he let Aaliyah's hand go. With my hand still in his, we walked to his section. I looked at Aaliyah. I was wondering why she had this weird look on her face. My eyes followed the direction she was looking in and saw her, and some fine nigga staring each other down. He stood up, walked over to her, invaded her space by grabbing both of her hands in his, and whispered in her ear. She blushed and stuff. Let me find out my girl wasn't as innocent as I thought. Then I was going to spank her for keeping secrets.

"Come on, nosey." Jam said, pulling me with him.

I didn't know who dude was, but I had a feeling my girl didn't mind if I left them together.

It was hot as fuck in the club. For the most part, Aaliyah and I enjoyed ourselves. I walked on the balcony to smoke a blunt and to get some fresh air. Aaliyah was in our section dancing. That girl loved music. I was glad she was having fun. Jam and his boys were shooting dice in the VIP area. It was like I wasn't even with him, but it was cool because I saw a lot of people that knew me and Tiger. Although I was out with another man, I still respected my relationship with my baby's daddy. Despite being tired of him or not. I wasn't trying to fuck Jam or have a relationship with him. When he approached me, I liked his style and the brief conversation that we had at the bar, if anything we could be friends.

I lit my blunt and took a toke. Staring into the city at the bright lights that lit up Hollywood, I cleared my mind of everything. I was enjoying myself.

"Damn, you never check your DM's? I been hitting you up." I looked to my left. Some short, thick bitch was looking at me like she had beef. I wasn't a fighter, but I'd shoot a bitch.

"Who are you?" I looked at her from top to bottom.

"I'm India. I'm Tiger's baby's momma. Well, other baby's momma." She gave me the stank face.

I burst out into a fit of laughter. Now bitches had been hitting me up about my man and stayed in his DM with the fuckery. This one was a first.

"Check your DM. You'll see the pictures. Now, like I told Tiger, if I don't get child support, I'm going to the tabloids. I'm telling it all. Someone would buy the info I got. Coke head, who is only with baby momma #1 because she writes all of his music."

"I don't give a fuck. You fucked a nigga, had a baby by him, knowing he was sprung on the next bitch, and now you can't get him to pay. That's your problem, bitch. It's not mine. Get the hell away from me. You are messing up my high. And I don't do coke." I winked.

"Aye, Momma. What's up?" I looked to see Jam approaching.

"Nothing that I give a fuck about." I looked at old girl. "Bye, hoe."

"Bye, hoe." Jam repeated.

"Fuck you, Jam. You are woofing but can't control your own baby's momma." She rolled her eyes and walked off.

I'll never let a bitch see me sweat, but I was burning up in the inside. I couldn't wait to get home to check my DM's in private. This nigga was pillow talking with a bitch about his business, and now she threatened to use it as ammunition. On top of that, cheating without using protection. Dumb ass.

Tokyo

The sun was going down when I arrived at my mother's house. She and Auntie Nita as I called her, were sitting on the porch. My Aunt Nita was smoking a blunt while Momma sipped from her cup, which I was sure was filled with beer. At 47, my mom was beautiful. We shared the same milk chocolate skin and nice figure. She had so many dudes checking for her, but refused to take dating seriously.

"Hey, y'all." I said somberly. After taking a seat on one of the empty chairs next to Momma, I let out a long sigh.

"What's the matter, niece?" Auntie Nita asked. Auntie Nita put you in the mind of the singer Fantasia. From her looks to the way she sang. Auntie spoke ghetto but she was smart. Even had a high school diploma a d college degree.

"Girl, so much. Can you make me a drink?" She told me she would and got up and went in the house. When she was out of earshot, I told Mama that I wanted her to send Auntie Nita home because of what I had to say. I wanted to do it in private. Now my auntie was with the shits like me and my mama but this here I wanted to keep just between my mom and me. Auntie Nita came out and handed me a glass with wine in it. She gave me a little shot bottle of Cîroc. I thanked her.

"So, what's bothering you, niece?" She wanted to know.

"Overwhelmed with business." I lied. We chit-chatted a little longer before my rude ass momma told her she wanted to spend time with her daughter. Auntie Nita told us she had a hot date anyway.

"Girl, that nigga she fucking isn't a hot date. His dick little as fuck." My momma said, as she watched Auntie get in the car. I burst into a much-needed laughter.

"Girl, you fucked her man?" I asked. I took a gulp from my glass.

"Shit, at least once a month. He paid. That's the only reason why I continued to give his little dick ass some play."

I burst out laughing. Momma was a fool.

"Ma, Jersey trying to leave me." I started. She cut her eyes at me. She wasn't a Jersey fan. She didn't feel he had enough money for me to be trying to claim he was my baby's daddy. I told her what was going on when I picked up the pregnancy verification from Auntie Nita.

"Wait, before you get started, have you figured out why the lawyer was trying to get in touch with Aaliyah?" I shook my head. I had forgotten all about it.

"She has not mentioned it and I forgot."

"Well, I tried to find out. I called acting like I was her and his punk ass wanted to do a FaceTime." I chuckled. "I know it has something to do with money. I just know your dead ass daddy ain't trying to do more for her than he is for you." I sat there for a minute and thought about it. I wondered if she was really hiding something. I had not really been talking to her, so if there was something she wanted to share I was blocking it.

"I'm going to find out." I told momma.

"Good."

Silence.

"So, Jersey saw a video of me and some dudes. Now, he's trying to say that the baby I'm carrying isn't his. He wants a DNA test."

"Girl, fuck him. I don't know why you want to pretend you pregnant by his broke ass."

"I love him." I told her somberly. I fought hard to hold back my tears. My mom stared at me. I turned my head. From the corner of my eyes I saw her shake her head. I burst into a loud sob.

"Cut it out." Momma came over and wrapped her arms around me.

Aaliyah – 1 Month Later

I was in a good mood as I cleaned my room while packing with the music blasting to the song titled, Love All Over Me by the R&B artist Monica. "Now I got love/ All over me/ Baby you touch/ Every part of me." I was going to spend my four-day weekend with my mom in Atlanta. While singing, I thought about my man. Jersey and I got through the drama between us. I learned why he was being distant.

He'd come over to pick up two duffle bags. On this day, I didn't go to class, so he assumed I was gone. He had a key to the house, so he let himself in. He was surprised when he saw me standing there, beating my face. I felt like playing in makeup that afternoon.

We made eye contact.

"You look pretty." He complimented me after he was over the shock of seeing me home.

"Thanks." I tried not to blush. Jersey was looking good in his gray tracksuit and fresh snow-white sneakers.

"Where's your car?" He asked.

"In the shop. My air-conditioner stopped working. You would know that if you would stop by or answer my calls." Before I knew it, tears were running down my face. "Jersey, is there someone else or is it that you just don't want to do this anymore? I don't get it." I was standing up. I watched as he went into the closet shaking his head. He grabbed his two bags. Walking back out of the closet, he dropped the bags and pulled me into his arms. I lost it. I sobbed into his chest. I was so hurt. I didn't even do anything, and he was treating me like he didn't love me anymore.

Jersey rubbed his hand up and down my back, which resulted in me crying even harder.

"Le-Le baby, stop crying. You're crushing me."

I was shaking my head. My emotions had been all over the place lately. I was crying at the drop of a dime and trying to sleep the depression away. It was all Jersey's fault. I even tried to reach out to Kash to get my mind off my man, and he had been short with me. He even canceled our last three tutoring sessions. What was wrong with me?

Finally, I was able to pull myself together. Jersey sat on the bed and sat me on his lap where he explained.

"I've been staying out of the way. I've been trying to keep you safe too. Trying to make the money to pay that nigga back has me stressed the fuck out. You know that I love you, though. I'll never forgive myself if something were to happen to you. I swear on my mother, there's no other woman. Just let me make this money." He tapped me on the bottom and I stood up. Jersey got up and stood next to his bags. "That nigga Kash cut me off. He ain't supplying me no more. It took a couple of weeks, but I found another connect. Things will be back to normal soon. Just sit tight." He walked up and pulled me close, planting a long kiss on my lips. He pulled away quicker than I expected.

"I can't wait until we move away." He shook his head.

I wanted to tell Jersey that I could give him half the money, or we could just up and leave, relocate to Atlanta. I would just have to graduate the following year at a new school. However, I wasn't sure if I wanted to do that. Jersey promised me he would call me. He grabbed his bags and left. That was almost a week ago. I was still sad, but I just let him be, like Tokyo said.

Monica went off the radio, and 50 Cent came on. 21 Questions was Jersey's favorite song. I went into my closet to grab a few items I purchased my mom but never mailed off, so I was taking them with me to give to her. The day I was with Val and the statement she made about what could be in the duffle bags that Jersey kept at my house was on my mind. Was Val right? Did he have drugs in the bag in my home?

Catch stunts in my 7-45
You drive me crazy, shorty, I
Need to see you and feel you next to me

I provide everything you need and I
like your smile I don't wanna see you cry
Got some questions that I got to ask and I
Hope you can come up with the answers babe...

I bent down and touched the bag, singing the chorus in my head. I unzipped it...

If I fell off tomorrow would you still love me?
If I didn't smell so good would you still hug me?
If I got locked up and sentenced to a quarter century
Could I count on you to be there to support me mentally?
If I went back to a hoopty from a Benz, would you poof and disappear.

"Oh my, God. Oh my, God." I couldn't believe it. Jersey had duffle bags full of drugs. I shot up to my feet. I couldn't get out of the closet fast enough to call him and confront him. He was putting me in a dangerous position.

"Aaah!" I screamed. Tokyo was standing in my closet. She scared the fuck out of me. With my hand on my heart, I snapped.

"What the hell are you doing sneaking up on me?" I shouted.

"Girl, calm down." I tried to step back, so she didn't see the bag but her nosey ass walked up and saw it. She looked at me.
"Why are you in his stuff?"
"Excuse me?" I raised a brow.

And when you asked me about it I said it wasn't me
Would you believe me? Or up and leave me?
How deep is our bond if that's all it takes for you to be gone?

Listening to 50, it sounded like Jersey was talking to me.

"I mean, if he's your man, then you should have his back. You know he can't keep the shit where he lives. It ain't like you didn't know what he was doing in these streets."

I stared blankly at my sister. Suddenly, she was team Jersey.

"Well, Tokyo. I'm not trying to go to prison and lose my freedom because of him. I have a future ahead of me."
"Well, your future includes a dope boy. Leave his ass alone or deal with it." She glanced at the bags before looking at me one final time. She turned and headed out of the closet. Tokyo stopped in mid-stride.

"Close that man's stuff up. Let's have a few drinks before you go out of town."

I took a deep breath, eyeing the bag one last time before I took Tokyo's advice. She waited until I zipped the bag before walking out of the closet.

"Get dressed I'm taking you out, crazy girl." Tokyo said before walking out.

Kash

"Let me get a hot link. I'm hungry." I said to my Uncle Stan, who was on the grill. It was a warm Saturday afternoon and my mother threw a BBQ for my sister. Our family alone was the size of half of a football field. The other half were friends and extended family. My mom and sister had been up under each other all day. She really missed her daughter and so did I. The three of were close. At 52, our mother could've passed for our sister. She looked younger than her age. Actually, Momma looked as if she was in her late thirties. She was a clean eater like my sister and they both took pride in taking care of their bodies. Momma was IG famous due to her famous outdoor workout classes. I had to check niggas my age for commenting on her videos. It was the same shit with Chas.

"Son." My momma called out to me. I was in the cooler grabbing a beer to wash my hot link down.

"What's up, Pretty Lady?" I greeted.

"Put that beer back and get a bottle of water."

"But I want a beer, Ma."

"Boy, put that gotdamn beer back." She yelled.
"You are an athlete with a promising future. You only get one body. Don't abuse it. Especially not for some nasty ass piss water."

"I put it back, lady. You happy now?"

"Don't get your ass whooped." She smiled.

"What's up, Momma? I'm about to go play dominoes. I'm up."

"I want you to spend a night and go to church tomorrow. Don't leave." She walked off without even giving me a chance to respond. Fuck it. Momma said I was going to church, so I was going.

I won like ten games straight on the domino table. If we were playing for money, a nigga would be up. I stood up and stretched. I looked towards the house and saw people lining up for the food.

"I'm about to go eat." I said to no one in particular. I stopped and hugged a few of my aunts on the way.

"Rich Man, Kash." I smiled when I heard the nigga call my name. It was Buddha. He was the only one who called me that.
"What up, fam?" I gave him a dab followed by a brotherly hug.
"Shit, you got it. I'm trying to be like you, boss man." Buddha checked me out, from my designer sneakers to my iced out chain. I did the same to him. He was dressed down in designer and even had on a Cartier watch. We both burst out laughing, something we did because we both knew we were *that nigga.*

"Let me talk to you, Cuzzo." I tapped Buddha on the arm. We stepped away from everyone.

"I fired that nigga Jersey. I heard about the fuck shit he did."

"Yeah, old bitch ass nigga. I swear I was going to kill him. The nigga paid me thirty racks. I gave him thirty-five days to get the rest."
"Damn. He paid that much?"
"Yeah. I pushed up on his bitch. I told her fine ass-"
Before he could finish, I shoved the nigga hard in his chest.
"What the fuck you sweating her for? She ain't got shit to do with it. Leave her alone."
"Nigga, you must've lost your mind." Buddha pushed me back. We started wrestling. Prison had him muscled up, but I could hold my own. I flipped his ass on the ground and got on top of him. I felt

my body being yanked off him. It was two of my uncles. One of my aunts called herself helping Buddha up.
"Y'all cut that shit out." My uncle warned.
"That's him. Fighting me over a girl." Buddha taunted and laughed. I didn't see shit funny. Jerking away from my uncle, I walked off pissed. Pissed at Buddha and pissed at how I was feeling Aaliyah too much. I hadn't talked to Juicy in a minute. I was trying to stay away from her. I wanted her bad, but I knew she wasn't ready.

Jersey

Pulling into the Starbucks parking lot, I killed the engine on my ride. Grabbing my gun from the center console, I secured it on my waist. Before climbing out, I debated if I wanted to go inside the bitch or not. I had a long drive and Starbucks coffee was the only one that kept me up.
'Fuck it,' I thought getting out. The moment I shut the door, a black Ford Explorer swooped up on me, almost hitting me. I didn't bother reaching for my heat. I already knew who the fuck it was.
"Mr. Nash, let's take a ride." Officer Frosty opened his back door.
"Hurry up, bitch!" He yelled. I wanted to knock his punk ass out. However, I knew that wouldn't be a good idea. I hopped in the back seat, and he slammed the door. Officer Frosty got in the truck.
"Man, I got somewhere to be."
"Oh, I know about you going to meet up with your man." He laughed. My stomach turned.

"You got me twisted. Miss me with that gay shit."

"Look, I don't give a fuck how many men's dicks you suck. That's on you. All I care about is you following instructions. I want Kash. I want that muthafucka and you are going to help me get him. Got it?"

I gave a head nod. What else was I supposed to say, if I didn't bring Kash down, I was going to jail. I wasn't doing time for nobody.
"I'll set him up. Just give me some time."

"Good. Now get out. I know you got shit to do and men to see." His fat ass laughed.
"Ugly, muthafucka." I spat before rushing out of the truck and shutting the door. I was woke now. Fuck the coffee.

Val

"Damn, it smells like feet in this bitch." I put my shirt over my nose to block the odor.

"You are going to stop disrespecting my momma." Tiger snapped. I didn't even see him or his nappy wig wearing momma sitting in the family room.

"Ain't nobody disrespecting your momma. I smell feet, shit."

When I looked towards Miss Linda and down at her bare feet wiggling her toes in my plush white carpet, I frowned and damn near gagged. Her feet smelled like stinky Fritos dipped in a dumpster of rotten garbage. It smelled worse than a homeless person who hadn't showered in weeks. Nasty heifer! She should've been ashamed of herself. I didn't understand how I was the only one who smelled the shit. I guess Tiger was used to it.

"Have y'all seen my baby's pacifier?" I looked towards them both.

"Val, you so damn rude. You walked in here and didn't speak, but talking about somebody's feet stink. You're embarrassing too." Miss Linda said.

"How so?" I put one hand on my hip.

"It's all over Instagram how Tiger's fiancé is cheating with some white boy." She shook her head. "You should be ashamed."

"Ma, hoes gon' be hoes. I ain't tripping."

"Hold up." I said putting up one finger. I ran upstairs to my bathroom. In the first drawer I pulled open, I saw my red scarf. After tying it around my nose and mouth like a robber, I ran back down the stairs. I was about to let their asses have it. They both were about to catch these hands. Stanky Foot and Dope Head had me twisted. Now I could tolerate his mama's stinky ass feet. Now, back into the family room with one hand on my hip, I looked at Ms. Linda. She looked up from her phone when she noticed I returned and shook her head.

"Miss Linda, now let's get something straight. You say I'm embarrassing when your son is over here going to parties getting coked up, fucking this bitch and that bitch. Got a ratchet hoe claiming she got a baby by him and how she will leak his cheating and dope problem. Now, that's embarrassing. Your son is a momma's boy with an addiction and a dirty dick."

"You better watch your mouth." Tiger warned.

"Boy, fuck you. You better watch your mouth. You are always on some disrespectful shit when you are the last one who can disrespect anybody. You cheated on me with a ratchet ass bitch and got her pregnant. I looked the bitch up and everybody's talking about how she tosses diseases around from fucking anybody with a dick!" I yelled. I was furious. I gave Tiger an ultimatum. He needed to go to rehab and get a DNA test, and if he didn't, there would be no more of us. We would raise our son, still do business, but that's it.

"Ever since she's has been messing around with that little white boy, she's been feeling herself, Tiger. You don't need her."

I stood there for a second looking back-and-forth at both of them, and in my opinion they both were pitiful. Yeah, I was still talking to Jam. We hadn't had sex or even kissed. However, our talks, whether in person or via text and our happy hour dates, was starting to make me like him more and more. However, I still loved my baby's daddy, and I wasn't just going to leave him without trying to fix us first. That's how my momma raised me. Speaking of my momma, if I told her how Miss Linda was acting, she would be ready to fight. She was one of the feistiest Puerto Rican women that I knew.

I would have never thought Tiger would allow the industry to come between us. We were high school sweethearts. Bonnie & Clyde. He came to me our first year in college and told me he wanted to rap. I was excited and encouraged him. When I heard his first three songs instead of laughing and telling him he was weak like his friends & family did, I waited until we were alone and suggested we write his lyrics together. I made Tiger who he was today. I had always been loyal, but now I was tired.

"I ain't even about to argue with you two, give me my baby's goddamn pacifier." I snatched it off the table and stormed out of the family room. Today, the baby and I were going out to Disneyland and Tiger was not invited.

Jam

That is one fine ass white boy, for a white boy, he is fine. That's a cute white boy. I heard that shit all my life. And although your boy was handsome than a muthafucka, the statements irked me. I fucked with black people all of my life. I know I'm white, but I identify with the African American race more. So, when I say this, I mean it in no disrespectful way, but niggas were prejudice as fuck too. A black person hardly ever told me I looked good or was handsome without saying "to be a white boy."

Looking at myself in the mirror on my living room wall, I admired myself. I stood 5'9, a muscular build, and my muscles were noticeable even with a shirt on. When I'm out the chicks don't just look at me. They stare and gawk. I rocked single braids; I have been growing my hair since I was a youngster. My blonde braids hung down my back. You never catch me without a hat. My head wasn't a funny shape or no shit like that, but I loved baseball caps. I heard I inherited my gray-colored eyes from my mother, but I haven't even seen so much as a picture of her, so I don't know how true that is. Rumor was my pops was Moms pimp. I don't know what dude looks like either.

It was Saturday, and I was on my way to a function the homies were throwing. I was going to go see my little girl first. I wanted to take her to get ice cream and let her play at the park a little bit. Today I wore a pair of red, white, and blue Air Forces, denim shorts that reached my knees, and a fitted Tommy Hilfiger T-shirt with blue writing. On my head was a blue L.A. hat. The three Cuban chains and fully iced out bust down watch made me go from simple looking to hood rich. I grabbed the keys to the Cadillac truck off the hook by the door and exited my townhouse.

I stopped at the gas station to get a couple of swishers. The blunt I smoked when I was getting dressed no longer had me high. I always had my pistol on me, so I didn't have to worry about grabbing it. Yeah, I was a felon and was risking my freedom if the popos caught me with a gun, but I'd rather they caught me with the burner than without it.

"What's up, Jam? You going to the Freaknik today?" A local hood rat by the name of MyMy wanted to know. I gave her the once over. MyMy was a bad little yellow bone, fine with a fat ass, but I wouldn't fuck her with another nigga's dick. I was surprised she still had all her teeth, how they say she was giving up hot pussy and smoking crack. A bitch burn me, and I was killing her.

"Yeah, I'll see you there." I told her and walked off.

"Jam, when are you going to let me take you out?" I heard her, but I kept walking. Bitch had to be high if she thought I was fucking with her like that. Back in my whip, I sat there and rolled up before pulling off.

When I pulled into the projects where my baby's momma lived, my whole vibe was thrown off. I hated that girl, and sometimes hated myself more for even messing with her. Don't get me wrong, I love my daughter, but Karen was a pain in the ass and some. I sat there for a minute, considering if I should roll up another blunt just to deal with her ass. *Fuck,* I thought, I just wanted to get the shit over with. My Air Forces hit the pavement when I climbed out, I was hit by the sun's heat. I spoke on my way to the door to a few people out.

Approaching Karen's building, my cellphone rang. Karen and her bullshit had me off my square. I fucked around and answered my business phone. I was off today.

"Yeah." I stopped in my tracks. I didn't do no talking in front of Karen.

"Aye, this is Jersey." I looked at my phone and wondered why he said that. That's when I noticed he was calling from a number I didn't have saved in my phone.

"What's up? You good?" I hadn't talked to him since I told him Kash was cutting him. He asked why, and I kept it real. To my surprise, he didn't even trip. He claimed he understood. It didn't make a difference if he didn't. The boss spoke, and that was that.

"Yeah, I'm good. I'll be back in town later. I wanna holla at you about something. Shit good too. Where are you going to be at around 10 o'clock tonight?"

"Shit, I don't know. I'll hit you up. I just walked up to see my daughter."

"Alright, but look, just to let you know, I got a new plug. Prices stupid. I know you and Kash would – "

I hung up in the fool's face. He knew the rules. Fuck he doing talking like that over the phone. I stood there in thought for a second, trying to figure out what that nigga Jersey was on. I concluded he just wanted to get back in, but that wasn't happening.

I wasn't even all the way up to the door and I could hear the music blasting. The door was open, so I could see Karen had her ratchet ass homegirls over. I shook my head. I walked right in the house and was hit by a funny ass yet, familiar smell. Immediately, my blood boiled. All I saw was red. I turned into the Tazmanian Devil. I slapped the first bitch that I saw, Coco, her best friend. She flew across the couch. I turned and was about to hit Pebbles, but she took off running out the door.

"What the fuck you hit me for?" Coco said, holding her face. She was still sitting on the floor. I walked up to her.

"Where in the fuck is Karen? Y'all bitches smoking sherm where my daughter lay her head?"

"I don't smoke that shit and you know it!" She yelled, getting up.

"Bitch, your god-daughter lives here. Why in the fuck you let it happen, period?" I guess Coco thought it was safe to get up. As soon as she did, I back slapped her ass and then dragged her out of the house. I wasn't worried about her calling the police, them hoes knew the rules.

In search of Karen, I walked through the small living room and towards the hallway. The hoe Karen was on her knees purring at my daughter, who stood there with her two fingers in her mouth, laughing. Moni didn't know what was going on. She thought her mom was just playing, but I knew. Karen was shermed the fuck up, stuck on stupid. I wanted to stomp that bitch out, but I didn't want Moni to see me put hands on her momma.

"Come on, baby girl. Let's go." When Moni looked up and saw me, she lifted her arms up so I could pick her up. Grabbing her and cuddling her in my arms, I looked at Karen.

"That's a wrap you can't ever see her again." She looked at me as if no one was talking to her. All I could do was shake my head.

When I walked out the door, Ms. Pearl was standing in her doorway. She looked from me to Moni and then back at me.

"Hey, Ms. Pearl."

"Hello." She said, dry and shit. I kept walking.

"Jam." She called behind me. I turned around and when I looked at her, she shook her head.

"You see what type of mother that baby has. It's getting worse and worse. You know what she does and how she loves to have everybody running in and out like she's running, a party house. You come over here get mad and wanna fight, but you ain't no better. You allow your daughter to stay in a toxic environment. I pray children's services don't show up and get her because the parents put themselves first." She slammed the door.

I took a deep breath. Standing there letting that shit sink in, she was right. I wasn't any better.

Ms. Pearl had a nigga feeling extra low. I couldn't stop thinking about how real her spill was. A nigga knew his baby's momma was an unfit mother. All Karen wanted to do was party and turn up. I didn't know she was back smoking PCP. Instead of stepping up, I tried to use force to make Karen get her shit together, all the while leaving my little girl in a dangerous environment. As of today, Moni wasn't going back. If she wanted to see her again, she was going to have to move out of the projects, go get herself together, and then she could possibly get Moni back.

I looked over at my baby girl, and she was sound asleep in the middle of my bed with her baby doll tucked under her little arm. I got her a few toys when we were out earlier and some other things since I left all her stuff at her mom's house. I smiled. The way she was making sure her baby doll was safe was the same thing her momma should've been doing with her. While Moni slept, I responded to my adoptive mother's text confirming me and her grandbaby would be at Sunday's dinner. Cherry Debose had no biological kids, but she treated me as if she gave birth to me. At six-months old, I was blessed with a loving mother and father. Too bad my baby girl wasn't.

I looked over at my baby. I leaned over and kissed her on the cheek. I made a mental note to call the home girl, so she could do her hair. Karen was a bomb ass braider, but she didn't take the time to braid her own child's hair.

Headed to the shower, I thought about the first time Karen braided my hair. We were in high school. I told Kash that I wanted to get some braids, and he took me to the projects. There I met Karen. She hooked me up. I got her number, and eventually she became my girl. Two years ago, we had Moni. She was pissed when she got pregnant. She said she wasn't ready for kids, but she knew that if she killed my baby, I was done with her. I will never regret my daughter, but I was warned. We were good until she felt like me wanting better was an act of me thinking I was better than she was. My hustling, moving out the projects and opening my car wash detail shop and smoke shop were for us. She didn't look at it like that. I tried, but she started messing with a clown who loved to whoop her ass. Said fuck me.

After a much-needed hot shower, I peeped in on Moni who was still sleeping. Grabbing my personal phone off the nightstand, I made my way downstairs. In the kitchen, I made me two sandwiches, grabbed a bag of chips, a bottle of water and returned to the living room.

Flopping down on my red love seat, I ate my food in silence. I wasn't a TV type of nigga. I preferred silence or a book before TV any day. I thought about how I was going to have to slow down in the streets now that I had Moni. My mother would have my back no doubt, but like Miss Pearl said, she is my child.

Chewing on my sandwich, I reached for my vibrating phone. A smile spread across my face when I saw it was Val. As much as I wanted to hear her voice, I let the call go to voicemail. I had to get a few things in order before I started back dealing with old girl. When I took care of home, I would come back for her. No doubt, she was leaving that punk ass nigga Tiger and I would be the reason. The phone stopped vibrating and right after I got a text notification. I had a feeling it was her, so I didn't even bother to read it. I really needed to fall back. For now.

Tokyo

"Damn, baby. You fucked the shit out of me. Got damn that shit was good." Jersey said.

"I always give it to you good, don't I?" Aaliyah replied.

"Fuck, yeah. But this shit tonight was good as hell." His voice was husky.

I stood by Aaliyah's room door, eavesdropping. My intention was to go chill with her in her room, and butter her up to see if she would mention that she was pregnant. I went snooping through her things while she was gone those four days. I did not really know what I was looking for, but still. Everything happens for a reason because she left her positive pregnancy test on the sink. I was heated when I found out that she was pregnant and scared to death. I hoped and prayed that she didn't keep Jersey's baby. If she kept the baby, I knew he would've found an excuse not to break up with her, and I wasn't having it. So, my plan was to butter her up. I wanted her to tell me that she was pregnant and convince her that she should get an abortion. I would tell her that she had a promising future and Jersey wasn't nothing but a dope boy. Aaliyah didn't believe in abortions, but I knew I could've convinced her.

Imagine my surprise when I was about to walk into the room and heard Jersey bragging about how good her pussy was. Mad was an understatement.

"Jersey, I gotta tell you something." Aaliyah said in a low tone.

"Talk to me."

"Ok, well. So, my mom's health is declining. I don't want to talk about her diagnosis until she gives me the ok. She wants me to wait. I planned to move there when school is out, but I'm thinking of going as early as next week. I will talk with the school to see if they can work something out, maybe allow me to do classes online. What do you think about leaving Cali earlier than we planned?"

My mouth was wide open. She was so sneaky.

"Hell, yeah. Let's go." Jersey was too excited about the situation.

"Yay! Ok. That's perfect. Look, I don't want anything over our heads. I will loan you the money to pay the guy back."
"Baby, where you going to get that?"
"I talked to my dad's lawyer. He said since I was graduating, I would inherit money that my dad didn't want us to know about. If his girls graduated from college, his estate would bless us."
"Wow. So, you giving me most of it?"
"I love you and plus you are my baby's daddy. I'm pregnant."

I stood there with tears running down my face. Jersey was yelling and saying how happy he was that Aaliyah was about to have his baby. I felt played by him, her, and my daddy.

In slow motion, I walked away from the door and to my room. I plopped on the bed. The first person I thought about calling was my momma. When she answered, I told her everything.

"Ok, so what you going to do?"
"I don't know."
"First, you're going to stop acting like a punk and figure out how you're going to have the last laugh."

Aaliyah

You took my love and I'm willing/There's no limit to the love I'm giving/The love I'm giving

Ooh/Oh yeah

There's no reason why we should be apart/Mmm, Oh, baby

Cause searching for something out there/ Will lead two lonely hearts, two lonely hearts

(Baby don't you know)

We come too far to let it all end/ I've told you over and over again/ How I feel inside but if you go/ Oh, baby, there's something you should know/ Something you should know

Michelle's old school jam blared through my speakers as I drove my Audi down the highway. It was a beautiful day outside, and I was feeling more beautiful on the inside because last night my man made love to me over and over again, catering to every part of my body. He confessed his love for me repeatedly and how I was all he needed and more. Jersey was so happy to be a father, and even happier that I would bless him with his first child.

I had to tell him to stop apologizing for the little drama we went through. It was behind us and from this day forward, it would be nothing but blessings.

I saw tears in his eyes. He made me cry. God, how I loved that man.

I headed to the school to talk to my professors and Dean about me transferring or even doing classes online.

My baby had a taste for some sherbet ice cream, so I stopped at the local Walgreens on the way and grabbed two containers of it. I was also meeting up with Kash to say goodbye. As a goodbye token, I got him ice cream too.

I pulled up into the school, parked, and text Jersey to let him know that I made it. He replied right away, saying good luck, and he loved me. I was cheesing big time. Love was a beautiful thing.

Before getting out of the car, I text Kash asking him to meet me at the library. I knew his class would be out shortly.

Kash: I'm about to walk to the library now. I'll see you soon.

His text alone had my stomach doing summer-salts. No matter how much I denied any attraction to that man, a fluttering heart, and butterflies in my tummy, and a wet hot box told on me. Although he was just a friend and I would never cheat on my man, I was going to miss Kash and prayed he walked away from the game before it was too late.

I looked up and over to my left, Kash had a strange look on his face as he stared towards the entrance of the parking lot. Whatever was going on got the attention of others. I proceeded to get out my car. People were looking my way. The flashing red and blue lights alerted me. Looking back at Kash, my heart dropped. Were they coming for him? Something told me to look behind me. Cops surrounded me. They were yelling for me to put my hands up.

"What's going on, what did I do?"

"Keep your hands up. Move away from the door. Do not turn around. Slowly, get on the ground." A white cop ordered.

The moment I was on the ground, I felt a knee in my back. I sobbed, asking what I did wrong. The handcuffs were put on, and they pulled me from the ground.

This was the worst day of my life.

"Aaliyah Monroe, you are under arrest for transporting drugs with intent to distribute."

What the fuck?!! I thought to myself.

TO BE CONTINUED- Keep Turning

And leave a review please.

G et Money - Two Years Later

"I got a play." Nunu whispered to a dude named Break. He was sitting in VIP, pretending to be in tune with the female entertainment. The whole time, he was looking for his next victim. As always, Nunu came through. Although Nunu would never admit it, hooking up with Break was going against The BGB code of conduct. She detested being sneaky, but she fucked up. What she and Break had going on was going to help her get it straight. The pair ate a few times off the plays Nunu orchestrated. Her cousins didn't know the real reason behind Nunu stripping at Club Slick. The girls thought Nunu was dancing because she wanted the experience for when they opened their own club. It was like she was an intern learning the business before they started their own, but that wasn't the case. Nunu had fucked up. Now she had to fix it.

Break gave her a head nod and threw up the number four. He secretly watched her as she walked away. Dressed in close to nothing with her lime green lingerie, Nunu made her way toward their mark. In four minutes, Break would be meeting her in the employee lavatory, so she could put him up on game. On the other side of the club, Nunu passed by Tone and winked. He was the young boss from Atlanta that she was about to score on.

"Hey." He pulled her by the arm, and she carelessly fell into his lap. Tone wrapped his arms around her waist and whispered something in her ear. She giggled and whispered back. He gave her a head nod and tapped her on the ass. When she got up, she looked back at him and blew a kiss. Tone grabbed his dick. He couldn't wait to hit.

"So, you about to trick on that hoe?" His God brother asked. He was sitting next to him with a bottle of Patron in his hand.

"It ain't tricking if you got it." Tone laughed and turned up the bottle of Ace of Spade. Boy Boy chuckled.

"The hoe better be bringing some friends."

"And that she is." Tone confirmed.

Nunu sat on the restroom sink and Break stood between her legs. His hands were planted on both of her thighs.

"Alright." She started. "He's from Atlanta. He and his boy are here on business and trying to have a good time." NuNu explained.

Looking into her captivating green eyes, Break rubbed her thighs. Break loved everything about Nunu. While Nunu tried her hardest to keep her feelings about him in check. She would never admit that she was feeling him on some 'you my nigga' type shit. She and Break rocked how they rocked with no strings attached, and both of them were cool with that.

Break never exposed his hand, though. His feelings were growing for Nunu. He wanted her all to himself, but it wasn't time yet. They both were young, risking their lives everyday chasing a bag, and turned up as they pleased. He didn't have the patience to try to get Nunu to be the girl he would have desired her to be. Which was out of the strip club with her ass at home and never ever risking her life for a bag. He would take care of her. One day, though, when they both had what they wanted in life, he would step to her on some serious type of shit. If they lived to see that day.

“I want you to be safe. Send the 'addy' as soon as you get there. Don't get distracted by the nigga's charm.” Break grabbed her by the chin. She took a deep breath as she gawked back at him.

"I saw how you were all up on him, smiling and shit. You were feeling the nigga." Jealousy was evident in his tone. Nunu wasn't lying. She respected what she and Break had too much to play with his intelligence. She thought Tone was cute, and after the thirty minutes she spent with him, they connected on another level. He was funny, a shit talker like her, and flashy. Yeah, she was digging his style, but she wouldn't admit it. Plus, her bag came first, fuck the rest. She learned her lesson.

Instead of responding to Break's assumption, she leaned forward and kissed him on his juicy lips. A light moan escaped her mouth when she tasted his meaty tongue. Break's hands roamed her body, turning the heat up between the two. It didn't take much for Break to have her hot and bothered. She was getting wetter by the second. When she felt his thumb on her clit, he had her gone. Grinding on his fingers, she found his belt buckle and began to undo it. Being that they were in the employee restroom and pressed for time, they had to speed things up. Break helped her by unbuckling his jeans and pulling his pants down.

"Oh, babe." She mumbled against his lip.

His thick penis was at the entrance of her hotbox. Removing her lips from his, she pushed the back of his baldhead toward her left breast. Break hungrily took it into his mouth. Shoving himself inside of her, they both cursed. Shit, she cried. Fuck, he grumbled. Together, they were in ecstasy. Break worked her pussy like only he could, and she gave him the wet wet like only she could. They would never confess it to each other, but neither of them could get enough of the other.

"It's so good. Damn, I love the way you fuck me. Please, don't stop." Nunu cried out from pleasure.

"Babe, one day you're going to be mine. I swear." Break confessed for the very first time-ever. Nunu's heart dropped. She was scared to entertain the idea of having a man after her first heartbreak, but Break's confession had her open at the moment. She tightened her muscles and worked her hot box on his dick. Break couldn't control it. He was about to nut.

"You love this pussy?" Nunu panted.

"Fuck, yeah." He groaned and exploded right inside of her. His head now rested on her forehead. They both gasped, still trying to recover from their intense session. Knowing they had to go, Break pulled out. "Make sure you get the pill. I couldn't help myself. I apologize." He told her, pulling up his pants. He was referring to the morning after pill.

"I will." She assured him. She damn sure didn't want kids. Break grabbed some paper towels. He reached over and turned on the water. Using the hand soap, he put it on the towels and then put them under the water. He handed them to Nunu, so she could clean herself up. He then kissed her on the forehead.

"Be safe. I'll be waiting for your text." He turned to walk out of the restroom. Nunu grabbed him by the shirt. When he looked back, she only stared at him. Her gut was telling her to speak what she felt, but then she didn't want to jinx what they had going on.

The feeling was sudden. It was a feeling she never felt before. The warning was so deep. *Stop. This play won't work.* Is what she was feeling.

Instead of telling him how she felt, she replied, "You be safe, too. Come back to me." Break smiled, winked, and departed out of the facility.

"IF I WAS A BOY" IS OUT NOW. IT'S A STANDALONE.

Words From The Author

I salute the strong loyal women who deeply appreciate the value and friendship of women on a much greater scale. It's been a long hard road to find liberation, and we cannot afford to fight our own gender on top of everything else we need to overcome. There is no greater gift than the loyalty and support of another Queen. Some have been conditioned to see other females as competition not allies, and to feel unworthy.

If we want to survive and thrive as women, we have to respect and honor each other enough not to hurt and betray one another. For most of us, the solution is about carefully choosing our friends and making careful decisions about the women we align with. For others there is more work to be done that begins with looking within to understand how to forge healthier relationships.

Envy is a very human emotion that can turn ugly if left unchecked. We are taught that how we look reflects our status. As a result, we will do anything to stay on top including betraying the women in our way. Let's turn the need for competition into collaboration. Remember, together we stand, divided we fall. In this book, you'll see how envy and the need to feel competitive can destroy families, friendships, and end relationships. In the end, the outcome isn't pleasant.

WWW.INSPRINGHOODAUTHOR.COM

www.ingramcontent.com/pod-product-compliance
Ingram Content Group UK Ltd.
Pitfield, Milton Keynes, MK11 3LW, UK
UKHW022015190726
13853UKWH00005B/1953

9 798478 511111